Loving a War Child

By

Loving a war child

www.celia-romanceauthor.com

https://www.facebook.com/celia.romancebooks

Published by Wise Owl UK Publishing

ISBN 9780956091772

Loving a war child

Having been awarded the coveted Autumn Best Read Award by 'Modern Romance', Celia's first romance novel, **Set my soul on fire,** resonated with passionate women around the world. A modern love story for all those looking for a timeless tale of life's greatest emotion.   However, Celia certainly likes to explore the unusual sides of how we love.   **Loving a war child,** is quite different from her awarded debut novel, this novel is no fairy tale. It is based around researched statements from war children who have been affected by horrendous acts of war and torn apart. How over time they are able to overcome the abuse, loss and hate to trust and even feel love again.

Celia said, 'This story has taken me several years to write. I found some of the research quite hard to read. It left me despondent for a while and made it difficult to express such emotional turmoil of what children went through.   These children are amazing and very brave, children have no choice about what happens to them. I feel they have very little support in helping them heal – and in some instances were actually blamed for what happened to them. They never get over it properly; how could they? Somehow, they learn to live with what has happened and move on. Children are precious gifts and should come first in all societies but unfortunately they do not. Soldiers who CHOOSE to become soldiers are helped when they have suffered traumatic stress. But we often ignore the impact of war on children, who suffer even the loss of their homes and families.'

Celia started her writing career by writing for children under the pen name **Lia Ginno.** She supports the charity **War Child**, as Celia's working life was with young children and teenagers until she retired.   Celia is giving 30% of the profit of **Loving a war child**, to the charity **War child.** http://www.warchild.org/

Loving a war child

Chapter 1

Yugoslav War 1991

The girl heard the snapping of a twig long before the two men came into sight and she wrapped her spidery fingers around the two knobbly grenades. Pulling the pin, she tossed the first grenade, tugged the second pin and threw the second grenade, which rolled swiftly after the first into the failing light. She watched as they limped along the mossy ground, gathering leaves as they went. Then she ducked down behind the tumbled masonry of a house and lay flat, covering her ears with her hands and pressing her slender body against the jagged rock. The shattering blast of the explosions made her head ring and lit up the Slavonian evening sky as if it was daylight. She knew before she moved that the grenades had found their target. The familiar smell of burning flesh and blood singed her nostrils and, in the silence that followed the blast, not even a bird or an insect moved as if the world knew too. She smiled inwardly with satisfaction.

Then she heard an agonised cry and her smile turned to cruel pleasure – were they still alive? After a minute, feeling sure that it was safe, she shifted and stood up, peeping around the rubble from her shadowy hiding place. Squinting into the evening air, she saw the dark forms of two men lying side-by-side like lovers on the gritted pathway. The nearest one was motionless but the other was groaning on the cold forest ground, his tattered body oozing blood like strands of red lace intermingling with the green combat cloth of his clothes.

Cautiously she stepped out and, bare-footed, walked slowly towards the still body and glanced down at the carcass of the first man. His legs had gone, his torso and half his head was missing, his entrails were scattered in bits about him and his one eye stared blankly at the darkening sky. She shrugged to herself, raised her eyebrows and smiled a twisted smile that was at odds with her big soft-blue eyes.

Low wails behind her made her do a swift turn. She moved a couple of steps towards the second man and peered down at the wriggling creature that was half alive at her feet. A deep red puddle had crept over her frozen toes; its warmth surprised her. She noticed that the man at her feet was caked with blood, which was leaking from the left side of his stomach. On the left side of his face the skin was peeling away from burnt black flesh, showing raw bone, and he had a lopsided eye and a comical smile. His right arm was still attached but shattered, hanging by a labyrinth of fibres from his shoulder and pointing towards the remains of his other arm as if asking to be put together again. Blood was pumping from his chest, jerking him like a puppet. His eyes were filled with bubbling agony. Slowly he became aware that someone was beside him, he managed to turn his head and focus his eyes.

To the half-conscious man the girl was a black silhouette against the dimming light – as black as the revenge in her heart. She bent over him and fear flooded his eyes like a tsunami. A girl with long raven hair that danced around her face like snakes in the light breeze was standing as impassive as a statue and gazing down at him. A mosaic of terror swept across his features; fear replaced pain, and his whole being wavered and shook like a windswept leaf. He knew who she was even though he had never met her. His breathing became shallow, his heart beat in his throat and he prayed to die then, for he knew what she was about to do; he had seen what she had done to his other comrades and he wished he had died quickly like his friend.

As if outside himself, he watched the girl bend down and yank at his torn trousers. A long sharp sword glinted in the moonlight as she pulled the deadly steel blade from its holster at her waspish waist. He cried out, startling the flocks of birds from the forest trees into a rustling screech. The girl flicked a look at him and smirked; then, with one quick movement, sliced off his manhood and held it dripping from her delicate hand like a piece of raw meat above him. Then, as if it was a tasty morsel, she stuffed it into his mouth, her eyes now on fire like the devils. She pushed it down into his throat deeper and deeper until he choked, spluttering blood from the corners of his lips. His eyes filled with water as he spasmed and his heart stopped.

Minutes later, the girl stood up and eyed her work. The two men lay on the forest carpet, each with his manhood stuffed into his mouth. It would be clear to anyone passing along the leafy track that they were rapists, but she knew that they were more than that, and that they had got their just rewards.

Leisurely, as though she was strolling along on a picnic outing, she went over to the heaped rubble of the house on the edge of the bombed-out village and picked up her frayed rucksack. Glancing down at herself, she became aware for the first time that she was covered in blood, her sodden clothes sticking to her body; at the same time, her brain registered that she could hear the cascading river that flowed nearby through the forest.

It was nearly dark now as she made for the river. Overhead the first stars pricked through the inky mass and began twinkling in the heavens. The moon's big silver face reminded her that, up there, the dead were watching her. In the beams from the moon, shadows leapt menacingly from each tree and shrub like ghosts. They did not frighten her; she gave a harsh, strangled laugh, throwing her thick tousled hair back and turning her face upwards towards the sky challengingly. Nothing frightened her anymore because she too was dead and her heart had frozen like a fountain in winter.

Suddenly she envied the two men she had killed.

Immersing herself in the river's icy water momentarily took her breath away, making her gasp. Slowly she removed her clothes, watching the blood drift from them into the crystal liquid like the paint she used to mix on her palette. Taking a deep breath, she sunk her naked body into the moving water, which gently rippled over her like arms of cold comfort. How she wished the water could wash away her memories, the nightmares that held her from sleep, as easily as it washed away the blood.

There was just one more man to find, the leader, and she quivered as his face floated into her mind. A face she would never forget. A man who lived in their holiday home town, who she thought was her parents' friend and an upstanding citizen. She knew where he had gone; to the coastal city, his family's home, where she too was aiming for. When she found him … And afterwards she would leave this torn country forever and seek her Devon home and grandfather in England.

Stepping onto the muddy bank, she pulled clean clothes from her bag and had begun to dress when a distant rumble of heavy army trucks made the ground tremble beneath her. They had heard the explosion! She knew she had to move fast. Grabbing her bag and slipping her grey tee-shirt over her head, she strode back into the middle of the flowing river. Dogs could not follow her scent in the water and she knew that they would bring dogs; she pushed her strong legs against the current and slung the rucksack onto her back. The noises of the trucks grew louder, then stopped; she heard drifting shouts … they had found the two men; she quickened her pace.

She was nearly a mile downstream when she estimated from the barely audible dogs' cries that the men had now reached the river. She flung herself onto the far shore and scrambled up the bank. She tore off her top and, naked breasts jiggling, trailed her tee-shirt along the ground up to about 500 metres into the woods. Then she rubbed it onto the ground and a tree trunk before casting it high into a tree, where it clung to a branch like a cobweb.

The girl backtracked carefully on her moulded footsteps and jumped back into the icy river. She was another mile downstream when she heard the excited barks of the dogs echoing with the music of the river as they picked up her tee-shirt's scent. She chuckled to herself – that would keep them busy for a while! – and continued to plunge her feet into the deepening depths, sending splashes of chilly water over her shivering body. Her legs were burning but numb from the cold and her lips had turned mauve.

When the river deepened the girl headed towards the shallower water near the shore, half swimming and half wading as the water started to swirl around her, taking her from the safety of the bank. Alarm fluttered abruptly in her chest like a fish caught in a net as she suddenly realised that the roar she had heard for the last ten minutes was a waterfall. The river was rushing towards it and taking her with it.

Desperately fighting the gushing water with flailing arms, she tugged at her rucksack, pulling it off her back as the bag was now carrying her along. Reaching into the bag, she tried to pluck out a plastic-covered pouch, but the drag of the water made her let the bag go. Swimming forcefully, she tried to regain some control and get to the bank, but a large floating branch caught her head from behind and the world began to spin. Water engulfed her mouth and hit the back of her throat with a sting; waves drove her head beneath the surface. Murky shapes gurgled about her, her limbs went weak and her body went over the six-metre drop.

Chapter 2

It was some minutes before she realised that she was still alive, lying on her back in the shallow water gazing up at the moon. She knew she couldn't be dead and wasn't in heaven because of the pain in her head. Surely if she was dead she wouldn't have been in agony like this? The pain wracked not only her head but also her body, and she had a struggle trying to remember where she was or what had happened. Then for a split second she saw her parents shot dead in front of her, and the memory of what had happened to her brother and sister-in-law a few days later returned. Vomit swelled in her throat along with water and came bursting out of her mouth like a dam. Eventually she found the strength to sit up. A burning throb surged across her eyes and again the world blurred. She lay quietly back down into the chilly shallow water, letting it lap around her as if she was flotsam.

Well, the girl told herself, you could die now or get up and find that evil bastard of a man. Her heart full of hate, she levered herself up and, trembling, locked her wobbling knees and moved slowly towards the shore. The moon was so bright that from the corner of her eye she glimpsed a shape bobbing about underneath the bottom of the waterfall. Her stomach twisted and she turned swiftly to face it, every inch of her body alert, but quickly recognised the shape as her old rucksack. With a small cry of delight she waded over to it and, undoing the sodden material, plunged her hand into the bag, ruffling around until she found what she had been trying to retrieve earlier. Her English passport and birth certificate, all completely dry, wrapped in a plastic pouch at the insistence of her brother.

'As long as we keep our passports we will all get back home to Devon and England,' he had told her. Tears blossomed in her eyes at the thought that her brother would never return to England and finish his doctor training. She shoved the pouch back into the bag and tossed it on to her back.

Gallons of water came hurtling down to beat out of tune with the stomping in her head as unknowingly she had drifted beneath the waterfall. Spitting out water, she gobbled in air as she continued to drift under the screen of the water. Looking up, which brought tears of anguish and a pain so sharp it made her cradle her head, she thought she saw a small cave-like hole in a rock ledge above her. If she could manage to get up to it she might be able to hide there for a while. Nearly drained of energy, her head pounding like someone was playing drums inside it, she hoisted herself onto a small overhang, nearly falling backwards into the river again, as the tumbling water knocked the bag on her back.

Somehow her hand found a niche and clung to it like ivy on a wall. Straddled across the rock, she felt her already tired limbs protest and shudder, sapping her remaining strength. Hot tears started falling down her wet cheeks. She let the rucksack slide to one side, pushed it with her hip to swing it around in front of her and pinned it to the rock with her belly. With the bag no longer catching the hammering water she was right under the waterfall and able to let go of her grip on the rock. With every bit of strength left inside her she forced her thin arm up to the cave ledge and, with shaking hands, hauled first the bag and then herself onto the slimy shelf.

The cave looked like a black hole with the teeming water shielding it like a dark curtain, but the entrance seemed dry. Cautiously the girl crawled on hands and knees into the pitch black, feeling the ground in front of her with quivering fingers, the hairs on the back of her neck standing on end, wondering if the ground would disappear beneath her.

About four metres in, the gloom gave way to rock as her eyes became accustomed to the dark. Surprisingly, the rocks were warm. Stripping, she took off her drenched pants and dragged out the few dripping clothes she had in her bag, laying them out over the warm rock. She curled up in a foetal position on the rough ground and closed her eyes, pondering whether the hard ground or the dreams of what she had just done would keep her awake. However, within seconds she was sound asleep.

The following evening the girl arrived in the large city that the river fed into. She had stayed hidden until late afternoon in the cave – partly through tiredness – and it had taken her another two hours to reach the urbanisation. An air of despondency clung to the city. Bullet holes traced their way across walls like graffiti patterns; rubble from shelled houses littered the roads; desolate silhouettes of burnt-out houses sloped at angles where shadows lurked and the wind howled like a demented ghost. Rats scurried into corners and dark trees were bending together as though whispering secrets. Men with covered faces and guns draped on their bodies were patrolling the neighbourhood. If they caught her would they guess who she was? Shivering, she pulled up her hood to cover her head, tucking her long hair inside. At least from a distance she would not be recognised.

The girl decided to sneak through the streets and find the city hospital. She was familiar with hospitals and the wound on the back of her head was still gaping. She could do with a couple of stitches if the hospital and doctors seemed safe and if she gave a force name it shouldn't arouse suspicion. If not, maybe she could hide in a corridor or in a quiet waiting room for the night. She moved through the city looking for signs to the hospital, and when she eventually found it she prowled like a restless animal around the building to see who was in there. As it was lit up like a Christmas tree she could easily peer in at the windows.

There was very little movement inside and no men or soldiers seemed to be about, so she stepped cautiously inside when she saw a nurse cross the reception hall. The nurse turned and smiled as she glimpsed the girl.

In the morning, the girl thought, she would look for the man's large family; she knew roughly where his parents lived, she remembered him talking about it when he introduced them to her mum and dad at one of his summer parties. She would quietly observe his family until she saw him or found out where he was.

Chapter 3

West Africa 2001

It was their eyes that made Doctor Daniel Kalu Williams think of zombies on the TV. Eyes like deep wells of gloom that held no hope; unreadable, dead eyes. They looked more like shadows than humans, lounging against the hospital walls aimlessly watching him. Watching every long stride he made across the gritty compound, every movement monitored in silence under hooded lids. Daniel had never been in a gathering of children who were so quiet; no chatter, no whispers, no curiosity, no playing, nothing; just displaced, dysfunctional children with clouded spirits in frail bodies. Some displayed stark bandages like white wings, showing the horror and the butchering that they had endured. It gave him the creeps and filled his eyes with glistening tears both at the same time. Nothing had prepared him for this.

Then there was the child – well, young female, but probably by the mileage of her life older than him. She had been tipped out of a truck just twenty-four hours after his arrival at the hospital. At first, the security guards standing at the barbed wire compound gates thought she was a bomb! She was rolled in a smelly tribal blanket that was sodden with blood and as she tumbled towards the gates she became covered with particles of red dust, like a patchwork quilt of blood and dirt. The guards, regarding her at their feet, had dropped their cigarettes, some preparing to run. They jabbered away, wondering if her belly could have an explosion in it and whether they should carry her quickly from the gates.

Then Daniel, wondering what all the fuss was about, had strolled towards the entrance and caught a glimpse of the child as some of the guards began to shift, frightened. She was nearly naked, her belly swollen, obviously pregnant and haemorrhaging badly, with welts and bruises over her legs and torso. Daniel could not believe his eyes when he saw her frail condition. He immediately gave orders for two of the men to pick her up and take her to his operating room. The men glanced at each other, hesitating, until Daniel, swearing under his breath, bent and scooped her up into his strong arms himself.

Daniel hadn't thought he could save her but somehow she survived; the baby died. When he told her, there was no flicker that she had even registered what he had said. Her eyes were as dead as the baby she held against her breast. After a while nurse Shani took the infant from her. The young girl had not looked at the baby once.

Now, as Daniel gazed down at her sleeping, she looked younger than ever, maybe fourteen or fifteen – she was a skinny little thing, obviously malnourished, so it was hard to tell. If she was in England she would be still at school and into the latest fashion or music. Nurse Shani reckoned she was a kidnapped child and taken by the soldiers as a 'wife' – probably gang-raped too. Rape was a powerful weapon here in West Africa, along with chopping off hands or feet; it kept people in fear and so in line. Daniel swept his hand over his shaven head, wondering what sort of animals he had come to help, and then berated himself for insulting animals. Not even animals would behave this way.

Daniel was a strong man of thirty-three, his strength hidden by his slim build and height of over six feet, and he was not used to making do. Yet here he was – the only doctor in a hospital compound surrounded by dust and outlandish equipment and the most outdated sanitary provisions that made him shiver with disgust.

Daniel lifted the child's hand and held her thin wrist searching for her pulse; her large dark eyes popped open. They were the biggest, saddest eyes he had ever seen and seemed to dominate her small face. Just like last night there was no fear in them when she looked up at him – she had gone beyond fear, beyond horror.

'Good morning.' Daniel smiled at her and the child just stared, her round doe eyes like limpid pools in shadow, making his skin prickle. 'How are you feeling?' he asked and thought, what on earth was he saying? This child had lost all feelings or emotions.

The young girl blinked, her long heavy lashes touching her soft cheek, and didn't attempt to answer. Daniel felt his guts twist, melting his insides; he wanted to pick her up, cuddle her, hold her close and tell her she was safe. Take her home to England – a land that had no conflict like this – and see laughter in her face, see her get angry for what had been done to her … anything to make her seem alive. However, he just sighed at her silence. Maybe, when she was well … Well! Anger flared, flushing his face and making his perspiring body glisten, deepening the sweat patches on his clinging damp shirt. How could she ever be well? Shaking his head with dismay, he thought she would probably join the other child zombies in the compound around the hospital as soon as she was physically well. As he stood gazing at her, he realised that, in fact, she was already one of them.

Later, Daniel found out that it was unusual for any kid to be brought to the protected centre and hospital. The people who worked at the centre were amazed; that was why they had regarded the child with suspicion. As he gently examined her – she passive and unmoving – his heart did a flip. Maybe this was it! Maybe this young girl had been left here just for him; she was the light that would purge his conscience for what he had done. It was not enough to just come here and help the country of his grandparents. This land was alien and distant in culture and scenery from all that he knew. However, he recalled that Mother Teresa had said that if you could help just one person in life … Would helping this girl be enough to wash away his sins and the memories that flooded his mind every minute of every day and night? How could he go about helping such a child; how could he ever make her smile again? Where could he start?

Finishing his examination, he pulled the crisp white sheet back over the girl's shiny black body. Her belly was as flat and smooth as any young teenager's. No one would have known it had recently been swollen with a child. She had not spoken since she arrived. Not even a groan had come from her lips or a wince of pain shown on her face.

'What is your name? Have you a name?'

Her eyes moved to his uncomprehendingly as if she had suddenly become aware that he was there. For a second Daniel thought that something flickered across her small face before she closed her eyes again and drifted back into sleep.

On the third day after Daniel's arrival, nurse Shani wandered into his small bedroom. She was a tall willowy woman, only a few inches shorter than Daniel. Her blue uniform looked clean and crisp against her polished black skin with no sign of perspiration. Daniel wondered how she remained so cool. You would have thought some of his ancestors' African blood might have kept his body temperature bearable. He had been laying full length on the bed, his door wide open and the small window opposite pushed open to the limit. The breeze flowing from the door to the window seemed to curl round the room, but miss him. He had even moved the bed between the door and the window hoping to feel some relief.

'Sorry to disturb you.' Shani grinned, her white teeth radiant in her lovely oval black face. 'The girl has spoken at last. I thought you would like to know. And the old lady, Lilly May, has died peacefully.'

Daniel sat up with an effort, feeling embarrassed at being found half naked on his bed. 'I knew it would be soon for Lilly May. I'm sorry.' He paused thoughtfully, swinging his legs over the side of the bed. 'What did the girl say?'

'Her name is Anneze and she is twelve years old.'

'Twelve!' Daniel echoed. 'And already had a child.'

Shani smiled and said softly, 'I was only eleven when I had my first daughter and my daughter was just turned twelve when she had Jobi, my grandson that lives with me here. I was a grandmother by the time I was twenty-two. My father gave me to my husband when I was nine and my husband gave my daughter to her husband at ten. It is the way and not uncommon here.'

'I didn't realise … you have a grandson here.'

'Yes. My daughter was very sick after her husband's village was raided. They killed her husband and chopped off my daughter's hands and Jobi's left hand. Unfortunately, she got an infection and never really had time to recover before the rebels came to our village; she was too weak to flee. She begged me to take Jobi and I fled with him and my two sons. However, Jobi was still ill from his hand being cut off and he would have slowed my sons down. They went on to the Guinea border with some friends to escape being forced to fight. It was two years ago; I have not heard anything about my boys but I pray that they are safe somewhere. I came here to the centre with Jobi and we have been here ever since.'

'And your husband?'

Pain swept across Shani's face and tears welled in her eyes. 'He was a good man and husband. He allowed us to escape while he stayed with my daughter and fought off the men trying to follow us. Another woman from my village who had hidden herself told me that he fought bravely. He had killed my daughter before they hacked him to death. Then, although my daughter was dead, they pulled her out of our hut and threw her warm body on the grass and raped her dead body before they mutilated her.'

Daniel felt vomit swim in his throat, but he managed to utter, 'you are so brave, Shani. I can't comprehend how you manage to seem so happy.'

Shani chuckled. 'I am happy because I have Jobi, good food and a comfy bed. I am not brave; you have no option about these things. I mostly carry the pain of the past inside me; occasionally it screams out. It is life here; Africa is full of violence and disharmony. Our history is about tribal warfare. We live with what we live with.'

And Daniel thought he had bad memories …

Shani saw misery flash across Daniel's features as she continued. 'I am glad for Lilly May; she had a long life full of struggle, she was old, and now she is at peace and happy.'

As Shani spoke, she swept her eyes over Daniel's half-clad body and shivered, her eyes alight. He was handsome for a white man, she thought; broad shoulders, slim hips and flat nipples nestling in a sprinkling of chest hair which intrigued Shani. It was all she could do to stop herself from stepping close to him and running her fingers through it. Very few Africans had chest hair. Instead she turned. 'I will bring you a special tea. It will help to cool your white blood.' And mine too, she thought. Shani had never felt this … knot in her insides for her husband.

By the time Shani returned, Daniel had had a quick wash with lukewarm water in the bowl on top of his chest of drawers and put on a clean shirt. He had straightened his bed covers, plumped up the pillows, pushed the bed back against the peeling painted wall and kicked his old battered case, still only half unpacked, behind the curtained corner that acted as a wardrobe.

As she entered, Shani smiled at the sudden neatness of the bare room. She placed the tray on the round table and seated herself on the only chair in the room next to the wrought iron bed where Daniel sat. She was very aware of his nearness, his raw male smell and the sexual energy that bounced from his slim torso. Pouring herself and Daniel tea which looked like liquid gold in the reflected sunlight streaming through the small window, she handed Daniel his cup, unconsciously deciding that she would have to brighten the room, make it more homely and … friendly.

'By the way,' Daniel said, sipping the ghastly concoction that Shani called tea and smiling to himself, 'my grandfather was African. I am considered of mixed race or coloured in England, not white.' It struck him how awfully English this scene was, sitting here on a Sunday afternoon with nice china cups – where had they come from? – and a teapot.

'Coloured?' Shani frowned.

'Oh, coloured can mean anyone that is African or Caribbean and does not have pure white skin.'

'Oh I thought you were sun tanned. What if you come from China and have yellow skin?' she asked, her eyes dancing mischievously.

Daniel saw the twinkle and wondered if she was teasing him, but not being sure he said, 'No, they would probably be referred to as Chinese.'

'Why, you have just said …'

'Yes; I meant I am referred to as coloured, not as white, because of my mixed race.'

'Coloured … Like paint …'

'Mmm …' Daniel decided it would be easier to change the subject. 'What else did Anneze say to you? Did she tell you what happened to her?'

'Yes. She was taken from her village by the soldiers that had butchered her parents in front of her. She thinks it was about a year ago. She was given to the commander as his 'wife'. He would rape her most nights and beat her regularly and sometimes he made her go with any new young virgin boy they took as a soldier. He told her he would come and get her after we had made her well. She is very scared that he will. So I thought you, me and nurse Dayo are the only ones that know what she properly looks like and that she is out of danger and will live. I think we should give her a new name. My daughter was called Adanna. It means her father's daughter, and because you have saved Anneze's life you are now responsible for her, like a father. She could have my daughter's name, and then we could place Lilly May and the child's dead baby in the earth. We will place them in the burial ground outside the camp with a cross with Anneze's name on it. That way she will appear dead and the commander or his men will see it and not come to the compound for her.'

'It is very disrespectful to Lilly May – and surely the rebel soldiers wouldn't come to the compound to get the girl, with all the guards we have?'

Shani chuckled, shaking her head at Daniel's naïveté. 'Lilly May would have been delighted to help. It was her nature. And the only reason the rebels do not attack this compound is because they might need the hospital's facility one day, or they might even want to take the uninjured children we have here as soldiers. The refugee camp that has grown outside around the hospital has some guards too but even combined with the compound guards they wouldn't stand a chance. The rebel soldiers are vast in number.'

'We are in a town – well, on the edge – and I thought the hospital and the camp was in a 'protected compound'. Protected by the UN. My work contract is with Doctors Without Borders.'

'Your contract does not state that you will always be safe, does it?'

'Well, no.'

'And where are the UN troops when you need them?' Shani asked, her eyes wide. 'Do not underestimate the rebels' skill or cunning. They have plenty of secret supporters and guards that they can bribe for information. Sometimes they come and rape the woman in the beach camp, and so do our guards. No, we live "protected" by the grace of God, not by earthly men … and one day …' Shani shrugged.

Daniel's face went pale enough to be classified as white by any white man's standards. He had thought he was safe; now, suddenly, he became aware of the fragile position he was in. No wonder there had been such a turnover of foreign doctors. Perspiration beaded on his forehead and his stomach felt like he had just swallowed a heavy stone. He heard himself ask, 'When shall we pretend Anneze has died, then?'

Chapter 4

It had been two weeks since they buried Lilly May as Anneze with a brief ceremony and placed an old wooden cross on top of the hard ground with Anneze's name carved on it. Anneze had then been included in the chaotic influx of several different groups of mutilated and injured orphaned children that came with fleeing women. She had been registered in the hospital as Adanna, and her physical condition had improved. She could manage to wash herself and get up each day after coaxing, and walked to the table to have her meals. Once she had eaten she would fly back to her bed like a bird to its nest and cuddle her pillow, curled up in the foetal position, oblivious to all that went on around her.

Although Daniel was rushed off his feet with new patients, Adanna haunted his thoughts. Even though he was surrounded by damaged children he made sure he saw her each evening, determined but still at a loss as to how he could help this broken child.

One evening, while Daniel was sitting beside Adanna reading to her and to the other children from a fairy tale book that had belonged to his small son and that now travelled with him like a comfy toy, they heard close gunfire. Adanna sat bolt upright, alarmed, her face like wax with fear. Automatically, Daniel gently took hold of her hand. It was icily cold but clammy. He murmured soothing words that he did not feel, praying that whatever was going on outside would not compromise the safety of him or of the camp compound or hospital. Daniel continued to read his bedtime story and stroke Adanna's bony hand at the same time. The other patients, mostly children, who had not dived under their sheets had got out of their beds and joined Adanna in or on her bed, fitting together like the close-set stones of a building, their faces like a corpse within it. The minutes crawled by like years, Daniel's voice a low hiss speaking with a uniformity of emphasis that made his words stand out like raised type for the blind. He had his head bent over the page to disguise the fear he knew would show on his features.

The door to the ward was flung abruptly open and every eye turned towards it. Shani stood there, her erect slim body silhouetted in the doorframe. 'Everyone OK?' she asked in a matter-of-fact tone. Daniel nodded.

'Don't worry about the gunfire; it is just some of the camp guards chasing a couple of thieves that have stolen food.'

When Daniel tried to continue with his reading he realised that the hand holding the book was trembling. He looked up at the children, breathed deeply and smiled, trying to regain command of his body.

'Finish the story then,' Adanna said to him as she lay back down on the pillow, her tight curly hair like muddy bubbles on a pond.

Daniel was so surprised that he nearly dropped the book. She had been listening to his stories after all, and she had actually spoken to him! With his taut muscles feeling more relaxed, he started reading again with renewed energy.

After that, Daniel's bedtime stories became a nightly routine, and most of the children would gather around him. He also found pencils and paper – well, not so much found as acquired them from the office store room, each piece of paper and pencil with a UNICEF logo – and got the kids that still had hands to draw pictures about each story and pin the drawings on the dull, unkempt walls.

He discovered that Shani could not read or write and had 'qualified' as a nurse under nurse Dayo, who was the only fully trained nurse there. So he found several women in the camp who could read and bribed them with extra food to come and teach the staff and children. He was staggered at how quickly the children learnt and at their eagerness, and he started a special reading programme for the child amputees.

Shani was so grateful about learning to read and write that she brightened up his room. First, a colourful tribal blanket for his bed appeared, then some nearly-new blue curtains for his 'wardrobe' and a matching tablecloth, both of which she had made herself.

One night when Daniel returned to his room he found that his walls had been freshly painted and Shani was nearly jumping up and down with excitement. Daniel was so overcome with emotion that he was unable to speak.

'Don't you like what we have done? It has taken us so much effort to get paint.'

Daniel's eyes glistened as he turned and pulled Shani into his arms for a hug. 'I am pleased, honestly; just greatly surprised.'

Then he realised that Shani was in his arms and looking up at him, not moving away from him or out of his arms. She felt warm and soft despite her thinness and he felt himself stiffen; it had been a long time since he had held a woman in his arms. Her eyes were as bright as sunlight on a stream; her smile filled the silence like speech. His mind hovered as if caught between winter and spring and, as he hesitated, Shani stretched up and kissed him fully on the lips. Daniel responded with a hunger that burned like a living coal in his heart.

Shani was astonished at the passion that swept over her as she feverishly unbuttoned Daniel's shirt and slid her slim hands into his chest hair. An endorphin rush as quick as a wild animal made her head spin and she felt unsteady as Daniel broke away from her mouth and yanked at her cotton dress.

Daniel had quivered at Shani's touch and he felt his racing pulse beat in his throat as adrenaline and desire mounted in his body. He dragged her flimsy dress over her head and stared, amazed, at her full heavy breasts. She had seemed so wiry and thin! He usually liked more meat on his women, but Shani's breasts were like plump black plums and had him mesmerised. He reached out his hand, cupped one in his clammy palm and, bending his head, engulfed her rigid nipple in his mouth, suckling it, her taste mixed with the scent of her skin intoxicating him. It had been a long time since he had touched a woman and experienced all the wonders of a woman's body.

The desire to bury himself inside Shani was overwhelming. Heat was flashing from her, just like him, and when he slipped his hand down and felt the hot, wet, squashy flesh of her insides, he was unable to resist any longer. He took her hand gently and they moved to his bed, where he pushed her down onto the crumpled cover and parted her legs. He shifted his body, drawing her narrow hips closer, and glided into her as blood roared in his ears. The desperation as he sunk into her velvet flesh made him gasp. Shani closed tight around him and he half withdrew and then thrust deeper in a giddy maze and nestled as if in a deep well of comfort. Shani let him. He focused on her quiet smile and pulled back again as she bucked. His thrusting speeded up as she dug her fingers into his back. He snuffled at her neck, licked the side of her ear and then sought her mouth, threading his fingers through the short cap of her braided hair as their tongues danced. Their bodies moved together, stirring the depths of their beings until suddenly they both burst, each with a cry.

Daniel was convinced that Shani was magic. How else could he feel so nearly whole again? Even the conditions in which he lived seemed better; not just his room where he and Shani would make love most nights until she returned to Jobi's bed in the early morning, but he even became adept with his antique hospital equipment.

When Shani was in the hospital he found it hard to take his eyes from her. She would go about her duties with such calm; she walked or rather glided around the beds in a graceful, soft manner like a beautiful black swan. She sparkled with laughter, bringing peace to all her patients. Her compassion knew no bounds. Slowly Daniel fell in love.

At first he felt guilty about his feelings, but he could not help himself. It was a different love to the one he had felt for his wife. It was more like joyous music or a gentle glow of stillness that lodged inside him.

For Shani, love for Daniel overwhelmed her every thought; their lovemaking was like a rocket that discharged a shower of golden stars. She felt as brilliant as the morning and could not understand why she had never felt like this about her husband. She had been sure she had loved her husband deeply, but her love for him now seemed as pale as drifting blossom. The only thing clouding her happiness was that something in Daniel was haunting him; she had seen it the first time they had made love and sometimes she would catch the same expression in his eyes at odd times of the day and night as if a drifting memory that gave him pain had floated into his head. She never asked about it. She thought he would tell her as the pain ebbed.

As for Adanna, she worshipped Daniel. She would jump out of bed as soon as he entered the ward and follow him around like a devoted dog, listening to his assessment and treatment of each patient. Daniel did this for the benefit of – and in consultation with – his two assistants, Noah and Tau. Neither were formally qualified; like Shani and the three other nurses they had been trained on the job. Noah and Tau had trained under numerous doctors; they were highly regarded in the camp and were called Doctor Noah and Doctor Tau. Daniel found Noah's skills as good as his – Noah had to be, he had been the camp 'doctor' for nearly six years as the hospital was often without any qualified 'foreign' doctor.

One day, when the ward was empty of nurses, Daniel asked Adanna to find a nurse, as he needed help changing a bandage. Adanna said that she could help. Daniel hesitated, but Adanna's confidence and her nimble fingers as she began to unwrap the bandage soon dismissed his worries, and so Adanna started her nurse 'training'. Within weeks she was competent with wounds and even helped Daniel and Shani one day in the operating theatre ... and that was when Daniel realised how he could help Adanna.

Although she was still young, Daniel knew that Adanna would make a good doctor, and he was determined to encourage her and train her for a future. He also decided to try and adopt her, so that when his time in Africa was up he could take her back to England. When he told her, she was thrilled and started to call him Papa, which brought sadness sweeping across his eyes as a memory flooded his mind.

Shani, on the other hand, seemed to get more and more annoyed with Daniel for talking to Adanna about her future. One night Daniel was sitting in his room waiting for Shani to join him when she flung herself through the door, her dark eyes blazing and her gaze so scorching hot she nearly caught fire. Daniel immediately jumped to the wrong conclusion. He threw her a 'big bad wolf' smile and, grabbing her slim hand, pulled her towards him. His penis stiffened and his heartbeat quickened as they fell onto the bed. When she pushed her hands against his chest, wriggled out of his grasp and stood up, he thought she wanted to play.

'Stop it, Daniel; I have words to say to you.'

Daniel was so surprised.

Glancing up at her he became aware that it was anger not passion ... and she was usually so mild-tempered except when she made love. He arched a brow and looked up at her taut figure and her face tempered like steel. Her penetrating gaze made him shift uncomfortably on the bed. His manhood shrivelled as fast as it had hardened and he could not for the life of him see why she was cross with him. 'Well, what's up?' he asked lightly, sitting upright on his bed.

'It is what you are promising Adanna. She is over the moon about you and her future; how can you be so cruel?'

'Cruel? I'm serious about her future.'

'How can you promise a future? We may have no future; tomorrow we could all be dead!'

This time Daniel took hold of both Shani's hands and held them firmly, looking up gently into her angry face. 'And if we are, she will have had a dream of happiness to the last moment.'

Shani suddenly nodded, her body sagging, only her arms held by Daniel keeping her upright. 'I never looked at it like that,' she said quietly. 'I never think about the future.'

'I've noticed and I can understand why.'

Shani's eyes swirled with glistening tears. 'I'm sorry.'

'It's OK,' and Daniel ran his finger across her soft cheek, catching a diamond dewdrop tear as it rolled down her face. 'Don't cry.'

Awareness zinged through Shani's body at Daniel's gentle touch and she smiled back at him helplessly. He traced a finger around her full lips, causing a sensuous shiver, and sniggered. Then she melted into his arms and they fell back onto the bed. She slipped one hand inside his shirt and he swelled to life against her belly. Slowly she undid his shirt buttons, kissing his chest with hot lips as she undid each button.

Daniel glided his hands to the top of her wrapped cotton dress and with a sharp tug he had uncurled it from her body. Cradling her cheek, he pressed his lips to hers, kissing her hard and desperately, their tongues colliding feverishly until Shani came up for air, her nipples pouting wantonly. She met Daniel's gaze for a beat as his warm mouth ringed her breast, sucking on it like a thirsty child. Prickles ran up her legs and nestled in her moist insides, which were throbbing with ravenous hunger. Heat, love and need took over her thoughts; words disappeared like a wisp of smoke as Daniel tasted her sweet soft mounds. Her tingling tips peaked and she thrust them deeper into the cavern of his mouth, her back arching and her hands clinging to his smooth head.

Satisfied at last with the taste of her breasts, Daniel glided his lips down Shani's belly, giving her fevered kisses until her body was covered with goose bumps and her legs fell open. Then he traced a path with his tongue from her inner thigh to the junction of her legs. When his tongue found that secret sweet spot, she had to bite back a groan. Her heart galloped in her throat and an orgasm pushed its way out like bubbling champagne that burst forth when it was poured.

Daniel slid his gaze up to Shani's face in time to catch her mouth twitch, her eyes dizzy with lust. Then, slowly, she moved her slender body from his side and sat astride his torso, tucking his hard penis inside her where she took it slow and easy, swivelling her hips in a circle, screwing herself down onto him, her long black legs like smooth beautiful jet in the moonlight. Daniel had helped himself to her body; now it was her turn. She rode him with the expertise of a jockey, tantalising him, provoking surges of sensuous torture until wildness took over them both. They yielded to the buzz of the moment through the riot of their senses and then came, quivering like harp strings until they were still.

As Daniel's heartbeat returned to normal he glanced at Shani beside him. Her big brown eyes were half closed like a cat and a satisfied smile was on her face. Daniel's heart filled with love and he knew he did not want to ever be without her. He also knew that it was time he told her; gave her a future.

'Shani,' he said softly, her name lingering on his tongue like he had just discovered the wonder of the word.

'Yes?' she turned to him and he felt her warm breath on his neck as she tucked herself into his side.

'Will you marry me?'

She was silent for a few seconds and then she propped herself up on one elbow and gazed at him intently. 'Do you love me?'

Daniel gave her a lopsided grin, pulled her down towards him and kissed her with such tenderness that her body began to heat up again. 'How could I not,' he answered, and swept his mouth down the side of her neck. 'If we marry, you will have to come back to England with me. I don't want to stop here where people butcher and kill children.'

'What about Jobi? I cannot leave him.'

'As if I would let you; him, too. I will adopt him and Adanna, if that is OK?'

'Give us a future,' Shani smirked, 'and even if it never happens we will be happy planning it.'

'It will happen,' Daniel said, angling Shani's chin to kiss her sensual lips just as a shadow of unease washed over him – or was it the ghost of his late wife?

Shani saw the melancholy and felt the chill, 'Why don't you tell me, Daniel?' she asked, grabbing his slim fingers and holding them gently.

'Tell you what?'

'Whatever it is that's haunting you.'

Daniel was silent, gazing down into Shani's milk chocolate eyes, and whispered, 'I can't. Do you love me?'

Shani gave a deep sigh. Whatever had happened, Daniel could not forgive himself. She could not imagine it was really bad; Daniel was such a good man. She guessed she would find out in time. It was just taking longer than she thought. Smiling up at him she ignored the dangling question that was like a seagull crying in the wind between them and answered the new question he was asking. 'Oh yes, Daniel. I never knew I could have such feelings.' And she saw the pain fade from his face.

'So why did you ask if I loved you? Your marriages here are not based on love, are they?'

'Some are, but most are arranged marriages. Your parents marry you to who they think will look after you best. But I know that in your culture love is most important for marriage.'

'And do you think that if your parents were alive they would approve of me and that I would look after you?'

Shani nodded.

The words nearly came to Daniel's lips then, but somehow would not come out. Instead he said, 'I have just under a year before my contract expires, enough time hopefully to sort out the paperwork for adoption and our marriage. I'll get in touch with the various authorities tomorrow.'

Chapter 5

Adanna was collecting the things needed for the wounds of the four patients in her charge and singing softly the songs she had recently taught to the young children on the ward. These were the songs she had sung with her brothers; the songs her mother had sung to her. Her thoughts had fallen through a hole in time and the songs gave her comfort as she recalled the good memories with her family.

Her heart still missed at least three beats when she heard loud noises, making her go rigid with terror, but she seemed much better on the surface most days. She now slept in Shani's and Jobi's room in a small bed her papa had painted for her. But each night she still thought the commander might come for her and she would pull the bedclothes over her head and squash her body up close to Jobi, whose bed she had started to share as soon as Shani went to see her wonderful new papa. Her dreams were so vivid sometimes that she thought they were real until Jobi woke her quaking body, a held-back scream bubbling in her throat. Then she would cuddle up to his warm skinny frame and he would nestle into her neck and she would fight back the memories until she drifted back to sleep. On other days her mind would wander and she would smell the commander and feel him standing behind her, but when she looked … Also she could not stop cleaning her teeth and scrubbing her body.

When Adanna turned from finishing her task she saw her papa standing in the doorway with a big grin on his face.

'What?'

'You're singing.'

'Yes – shouldn't I?' Alarm crossed her sweet little face.

Daniel smiled down at her, scooped her into his arms and lightly kissed the top of her head. 'I think you should sing all the time. Your voice is so beautiful, as beautiful as you.'

Adanna wriggled further into Daniel's chest, delighted with his praise. She felt so safe, so cherished, when he held her against him, like she had with her birth father, although it had taken until recently for her to let anyone touch her or hold her close. It was not like the commander's rough hold as he pinned her down on the ground and rammed himself into her. The commander smelt of sweat and beer and sometimes the stench of dried blood, which clung to his clothes. He rarely took his clothes off even when he took her. He would just undo his trousers and his penis would poke out big and hard and aiming for her. Then, according to his mood, he might beat her for not 'participating' properly or insist on 'special' sexual pleasures to satisfy him.

Adanna had forgotten how gentle men could be until she met her new papa, and then she remembered her birth father and how he had always stopped her brothers from playing roughly with her. And now she was going to England, away from here and the commander and where she would go to school so that when she was old enough she could become a doctor. Her parents would have been so proud of her; in fact, since she had come to the hospital she was slowly becoming proud of her abilities and who she was again. She no longer felt as though she was not worthy because of what had happened to her. Like her doctor papa said, she was incredibly strong to have gone through such treatment and still have a caring heart. However, she no longer wanted a husband or a family like before. She would be a doctor and only a doctor and dedicate herself to her work.

If Daniel could have read Adanna's mind he would have been upset by how she saw her future. He was understanding, but he would not have fully understood, as he thought he had made more progress with her then that. To Daniel, love, a family and children were everything.

Adanna rarely flinched when someone raised their arms near her now, and she loved Daniel to come close and cuddle her or just hold her hand. Only five months ago she had been so distant, quiet and subservient. He saw confidence and trust grow in her again, especially since he told her he was going to adopt her and take her back to England and send her to school because she learnt so fast and was clever. After numerous phone calls he had just received some of the necessary papers and had started questioning Shani for the information he needed to fill in the forms.

Even Shani was excited, despite herself, about going to England and being Daniel's wife. Every night after they had made love she would ask him to tell her about his life in London and what kind of life they might have together. She said they were like fairy tales.

One afternoon Daniel and his 'family' went down to the sea, which was about half a mile behind the hospital, as a treat for Adanna's thirteenth birthday. They took both guards and some of the hospital children, threading their way through the waving wooded palms and the camp tents scattered underneath the palms like ant hills. Within ten minutes, much to Daniel's amazement, the children seemed to come to life, giggling and splashing each other. Adanna was no different. She had lost that hesitant and anxious look, the alertness to every movement around her and every rustle from the whispering palms and bushes, which she had had when they first made their way outside the compound with her gripping Daniel's hand like a lifeline.

She did take a while to relax compared with everyone else, standing for a time gazing at the other children playing on the sugar-white sand, then giggling at Shani and Jobi when Jobi splashed her with sea water. But eventually she joined them, rolling about alongside the other kids in the shallow waves while Daniel chased them, catching them and swinging them high into the air.

Since Daniel had started his reading and drawing programme he had noticed how the children were gradually changing. He was sure it was giving them something to do, something to achieve, but it was nothing like the laughter that rung out across the sand that day. It dawned on him that he too felt happier and freer away from the little world of the hospital and compound. The whole hospital environment was claustrophobic; cloaked in fear that hung over them all like a black cloud. He promised himself to set up a rota and bring each of the children down to the beach at least once a week; it was better medicine than anything he had to offer.

That night Daniel and Shani made love slowly, tenderly, not as though it was Shani's last moment. They kissed lightly at first, their lips pressed against each other's, then their kisses deepened until their tongues flicked and gouged at each other's mouth. Daniel's gentleness was so seductive as he slid his kisses over Shani's eyelids, ears and mouth, that she felt she had been plugged into an electric socket.

Daniel gazed into her big brown eyes and gave a wicked grin. She felt his erection hard against her body and her nipples went hard too. She felt his warm breath on her neck. He kissed the soft black sheen of her throat where the moonlight bounced off her sleek dark body like glittering sparks from an anvil. Unable to resist her smooth skin, he showered kisses across her belly, lust building and intoxicating him until he was delirious. His hand reached down for her magic spot and sought it with his fingers. She was already wet and slick with need and when he began to rub she started to squirm, a small whimper escaping from her mouth. He found a peaked nipple with his tongue and traced around it, licking it until she arched, pushing her breast fully into his mouth. After sucking he began nibbling at her nipple until she lay still, enjoying the sensations that pricked her body inside and out.

Daniel shifted from Shani's side and climbed on top of her, holding his weight on his forearms, slipping himself into the warm well of her femininity. At the same time he turned to her other breast and slowly swirled his tongue around her pouting nipple. She shuddered underneath him and her legs gripped his hips like a vice, pulling him deeper inside her. Fusion zinged through Daniel and tingles swept up his legs into his stomach as he pumped himself into Shani, his passion intense and all-consuming.

Even though he could still taste her breasts on his tongue, he took one look at her beautiful body lying satisfied beside him and wanted her again. Her body drew him like a magnet, an enchanting magic magnet that held him spellbound night and day. He knew that Shani felt the same, for she never refused him. She was the most un-shy experimental woman he had ever made love to. He pushed himself up on one elbow and rubbed his thumb across her full bottom lip, making her raise her eyes to his face, smiling that mysterious grin of hers that had blood rushing straight to his groin. The whole woman was a mystery; a wonderful mystery of sorcery and allurement. Daniel shuffled across the bed, bent his head and kissed the tip of her nose and Shani erupted into giggles.

'What?' Daniel asked.

'That was so tame! Was that my goodnight kiss?'

'If you're tired.'

'Mmm, tired. Shall I give you my goodnight kiss?'

'Not if you *are* tired and want to go to sleep.'

Again Shani giggled and snaked her arms around Daniel's neck, stretching up to meet his face, her lips twitching. She gave him a lingering kiss, pushing her tongue into his mouth, and he pulled her body into his embrace and held her like a captured animal in his arms. His whole frame awakening and on red alert, he knew Shani could feel how awake he was.

Still she teased. 'Goodnight,' she whispered into his ear, a soft waft of breath curling, tickling and sending unruly shivers down his spine, his penis so hard it was in danger of bursting. He began to stroke her, stroking her back and cradling her bottom, sliding his lips down her neck until she grabbed hold of him and lodged him inside her up to the hilt. Breathing hard he held her there.

'Don't move yet, I'll come too quickly.'

Shani let out a groan, her eyes black with desire, and shifted her hips cautiously. Daniel's fingers burrowed into her dark curly nest to find her clitoris, rubbing her gently as, belly against belly, he thrust slowly and relentlessly in agonised thrusts until he felt he was drowning in her. With waves of pleasure wracking his body he exploded, taking Shani with him.

Shani curled into Daniel's side, her head on his chest, each of them trying to regain some control over their breathing. He had had a good day, mused Daniel; the whole day had been pleasurable, but he could not wait to return to England. He was finding it harder every day to operate on the butchered children. Just as his eyes closed to dream that he was back home, the bad memories replaced by Shani and his new family, he realised that Shani was talking to him.

'Sorry,' he said. 'What did you say?'

'Today reminded me of playing with my sons. I wish I could somehow find out if they are safe and made it to the border refugee camp or what has happened to them if not.'

Daniel tightened his hold around Shani's slim body. 'Maybe we should get in touch with the Red Cross or the refugee agency. Both can help find displaced families.'

'How?'

'I have got the international phone number for the Red Cross. I will phone them tomorrow and register your boys if you give me all the details. They will also put us in touch with all the agencies that can help find them.'

'Oh, Daniel!' Shani kissed Daniel excitedly on his lips and eyes and neck.

'Hey, don't start that or we will never get any sleep.'

Chapter 6

It was amazing how the children in the compound had become kids again. They were as mischievous as monkeys and Daniel often had to watch where he sat or stood. He opened doors with caution after they balanced a bucket of water on top of a door and drenched him when he opened it, much to their delight and laughter. He had become aware of the signs now; first the hands and muttering, then the tittering of giggles behind the hands, as though they were telling secrets when Daniel passed. He knew, then, that he would need to be careful. Sometimes he deliberately let them win and other times he would 'innocently' avoid the prank.

The beach trip was now a part of the daily routine. The women from the tented camp often cooked food and made sweets after Daniel had acquired special 'rations' from the weekly UN helicopter visit; the whole thing became like a Sunday afternoon picnic and nearly normal.

Daniel was also only one step away from fully adopting Adanna and Jobi – and he and Shani had arranged a wedding date. All the children, hospital and camp were excited about it and were helping to prepare a feast, flowers and a dress for Shani. Daniel was only three months away from the end of his contract and, although he pretended that he would be sad to leave, deep down it could not come quickly enough for him.

Three weeks before the wedding Noah, returning one late afternoon from the town, came rushing into the hospital to find Daniel and the staff. He was perspiring and beads of sweat were glistening on his face, a most unusual occurrence for the calm Noah. Daniel, who was lounging against the wall with Shani in the corner of a ward listening to Adanna read to the little children, sprung up in alarm.

'Are you unwell?' Daniel said, striding quickly to Noah.

'No, no, I'm fine; can I speak to you for a moment in the office? And you, Shani; and Tau, you too.'

Daniel raised an eyebrow, then turned to Adanna. 'Finish reading to them, then Nurse Dayo should be along with their tea if you could help with that until we get back.'

Adanna nodded but her eyes held Daniel's for a beat as he turned to follow the others to the office. As he seated himself in a chair he noticed how rigid Shani and Tau were, and as he gazed up at Noah's terrified face he heard gunfire and a distant explosion.

'It's the rebels. They have entered Freetown and are heading this way. I was with my brother and he is arranging for as many boats as possible to come to the beach and take the women and children.'

'Is that necessary?' Daniel asked. The phone on his desk rang, making them all jump. He picked it up with hands that were shaking. 'Yes, Doctor Daniel Kalu Williams.'

'This is Field Marshal Appleton. I understand that Freetown is under siege, so we are evacuating all British personnel and their families. A helicopter is on the way to pick you up. It should be there in about fifty minutes on the beach behind the hospital. It won't be able to wait so please make your way there at once.'

'What about the staff and children?' Daniel asked as realisation dawned.

'They will have to take their chances until our troops arrive. Tell them to try and find a place of safety. We are sending five helicopters full of troops but they will not be there for two or three hours. Good luck to you all.'

Daniel sank further into his chair like a deflating bag; good luck, echoing in his ears. Surely, he thought, this must be a nightmare! The other nightmare that he had had before he came had nearly been chased away in his memory. He stared up at the three people looking down at him.

'Well?' Noah asked.

'That was Field Marshal Appleton. He is sending troops here, but they will not be here for another two or three hours. He said you must try and find a safe place to hide until then.'

'Then, will be too late,' spat Noah. 'Tau, get the children ready, and Shani, go down and alert the women and children in the camp. There is an underground cellar in the remains of that old church between here and the beach – some of them could hide down there if there is not enough room in the boats. The children will be loaded onto the boats first. If we can get far enough away from the shore we might be able to hold out until the troops get here. Now move!'

'Shani stays with me,' said Daniel awkwardly. 'They are sending an advanced helicopter for me and my family.' He felt like a coward running away, but he *was* a coward; he wanted to get as far away as he could as quickly as possible with Shani, Adanna and Jobi and have the fairy tale life they had all planned. He loved everyone in the hospital, patients and staff, and half of him would be sad and miss them, but he had had enough. It was all too raw, too evil for him to cope with.

Suddenly he was in Noah's embrace. 'Good luck, my friend. You have been more than a doctor and we thank you and I wish you and Shani a happy life. Quickly now, we must say our goodbyes.'

There was a lump in Daniel's throat and he felt guilty about his thoughts as he hugged Noah and Tau.

'I'll go and get Jobi and Adanna,' Shani said, her eyes glistening as she turned from hugging her friends.

'I'll go and collect the papers and passports. They are in my room. I'll meet you in the entrance hall,' said Daniel, opening the door to a sea of waxen faces. Adanna, who was standing in the front of the other children, was shaking like the ground before an earthquake. Daniel grasped her trembling hand and put a comforting arm around her shoulders, thinking that he too could do with an arm of comfort. The fear that was churning in his stomach was making him feel sick, and he knew it showed on his face. Holding Adanna against him, he smiled and was about to speak to the children when more gunfire was heard, nearer this time.

Swallowing hard, he said, 'OK, I need you all to line up so that we can go down to the beach. Doctor Noah is going to take you on a boat ride. Won't that be fun? Marcia, you and the other five older children, go with Doctor Tau and Nurse Dayo and help carry those that are too weak to walk.'

Noah put a hand on Daniel's shoulder, 'Go and get your papers, my friend. I will manage this.'

Daniel nodded gratefully and, still grasping Adanna's hand, disappeared out of the building across the dusty courtyard and headed to his room. Once there, he raced about tossing things into a bag. 'This will teach me to keep things in order,' he smiled at Adanna, who was rigid as a rod with nerves. 'Come on, let's go and find Shani and Jobi. We have a special helicopter coming for us.' Daniel held out his hand and, as if this news had melted the rod in her back, Adanna moved, gave him one of her famous wide grins, clasped his firm hand and together they went across to the hospital entrance hall, where Shani and Jobi were sitting nervously.

'Ready?' Shani asked, standing up when Daniel nodded. She picked Jobi up and Daniel let go of Adanna's hand and took Jobi from her. Shani glanced at Adanna. She had stopped dead. Her features were panic-stricken and her big round eyes seem to roll like marbles in her little oval face when Daniel let go of her hand.

Shani clutched hold of Adanna's thin hand in hers, patting it gently as they made their way outside. The noise of gunfire, loud blasts, shouts and screams was now clearly audible as they twisted their way through the palms and collapsed ragged empty tents. Pots and pans were scattered across the gritty sand and the smell of burning food left on the fires sailed through the air.

They soon caught up to the crocodile of fleeing children and staff, and, as they emerged through the palms and came out onto the beach, Daniel was flabbergasted at how many boats of various sizes were bobbing about at the water's edge. Already they were ferrying the children out to the larger boats further offshore.

'You three wait here, under the palm; I'll go and help,' Daniel commanded, and all three sat obediently on the warm sand. Then Daniel saw their scared faces and added, 'The helicopter will be here any minute. Look out for it.'

Daniel waded into the sea, helping Noah and Tau with the terrified children, lifting them up with reassuring words and placing them in the boat. Although it was pandemonium for a while, the boats were all filled and left the shore, some rocking dangerously with their loads. Daniel stood for a minute, his hand held against his forehead, watching the boats get further away and wondering where the damn helicopter was. By the anxious looks on Shani's and Adanna's beautiful black faces he knew that they were wondering too, and abruptly he wished he had sent them to safety out across the sea. Now they were trapped.

It was another silent minute between them, listening to the nearing rebel noise, before they heard the drone of the helicopter. They all heard it at once and twisted their heads up to the blue sky as the bird-like dot became a helicopter. Daniel scooped Jobi up into his arms and watched the helicopter land with a soft thud, its whirling blades swirling up the sand, which blew towards the waiting four. They shielded their eyes and bent their bodies as they struggled against the wind towards the helicopter.

'Doctor Kalu Williams,' someone shouted at them through the noise of the engine and blades. A man with a grey beard and unruly hair was standing at the open door and Daniel shouted back, 'Yes, that's us,' as gritty sand flew into his mouth.

'I'm sorry sir, we only have orders to pick you up. As you see we are full to the brim,' said a second man, a shimmering mountain of muscle and flesh, who yelled down to Daniel.

'This is my wife and family,' Daniel said, throwing first the bag and then Jobi into the helicopter. He swung round, grabbed Adanna and tossed her up into the compressed sea of bodies. 'I am not leaving them behind. Find some room. Adanna, grab hold of Jobi.'

'I wish I could find the room, but I have another six to pick up.'

The big solid man was beginning to irritate Daniel, looming in the doorframe. Who did he think he was: God? A whistling sound flew past Daniel's ear and a bullet hole appeared in the metal body of the helicopter. Shouts and startled screams were heard from inside the helicopter and it began to move. Daniel jumped on board and, lifting his gaze, saw rebels bursting out of the palms. The helicopter began to hover, and the two men were now trying to move him and close the door.

Crouching in the doorway, Daniel held out his strong hand to a trotting Shani, who was running alongside through the storm of sand in a vain effort to keep up. 'There is room for one more,' Daniel flung over his shoulder. 'Grab my hand, Shani; grab my hand.'

A shower of bullets spluttered into the sand inches behind Shani like the plops of large raindrops, then another fierce round hit the helicopter door and someone gasped behind Daniel as a bullet struck them. Then something hit the back of Daniel's head, a searing pain swept across his eyes and the world went black.

Chapter 7

Two years later: 2004

Daniel lay watching the grey English morning sky from his bed, his hair tousled on the pillow, willing the day not to start as the slow memory crept like a cold worm into his brain. He felt an undefined sadness as depressing as the dark impenetrable clouds above. He knew he was becoming worse, unable to shift the melancholy; the guilt grew harder to bear every day until even getting out of bed was an effort. He would not have bothered at all if it was not for the children. He knew he needed help; he needed some sort of counselling and so did Adanna.

It was just over two years since that horrific day in Africa. He had spent a numb, restless couple of weeks in Guinea during which he tried to go back to find Shani, but the area was declared a war zone and he could not get anyone to take him, even for a bribe. At one point he had considered driving himself back, but he knew that he would be lucky to get there alive, and then what would happen to Adanna and Jobi? They were already in a bad mental state. Both had been afraid to have him out of their sight. They even slept with him at night, curled up like limpets on each side of him.

It was a year before he stopped phoning the Red Cross and the UN for information about Shani, and he had eventually accepted that she would never be found, certainly not alive. He had heard that Noah and Tau and most of the children had been saved. If only they had all gone with them! But he had been too stubborn – too keen to get out of there and come back to England. He was to blame for Shani's death, just like he was to blame for the death of his wife.

Adanna had told him what had happened after he was knocked unconscious. She had squeezed herself to the window and seen Shani shot in the back. She saw her fall and, in a flat, dead voice, added, 'Even if she had not died then, she would probably have been hacked to death when the rebels found her. 'Daniel could not allow himself to conjure up that image, even now, because his entire body would be without air.

After Daniel had come slowly out of the haze of unconsciousness he had pounded the man that had been in the helicopter doorway like a power drill along with verbal abuse, yelling that he was responsible for murdering Shani. He would have certainly killed him if someone had not dragged him off and held him tightly. He still felt the hot tide of rage roar through him like a mountain torrent when he thought about it.

He crawled unwillingly out of the warm bedclothes and slid his feet into his slippers, shuffling to the window like an old man. He gazed out at the East Sussex landscape beyond the back garden. The desolate hills rolled across the horizon like a solid green wave; the greenest of green grass swayed in the paddocks where several horses grazed, just behind his colourful flowering garden.

Glancing down to the patio, he noticed that it was shiny wet in the pale morning light. It had obviously rained during the night, but he had not heard it after taking the sleeping tablets. Only drugged sleep gave him any respite from his memories and from the black pit of misery where he missed Shani with every beat of his heart. He thought how unfair life was; first the loss of his wife and child that had numbed him until he met Shani and then ...

As he stared unseeingly at the patio, a movement below caught his attention. He saw Jobi watering his small patch of garden and despite everything he smiled to himself. Didn't the kid realise that the earth was damp already? Jobi had blossomed since they had moved from London, and the fact that he only had his right hand never stopped him from doing anything. He was a tough little kid, like Shani, Daniel thought.

They had only been back in England for two weeks when a child had spat at Jobi as Daniel settled him back in his pushchair after visiting a potential school for Adanna. Luckily Jobi was too young to understand, but if Adanna had been with them she would have been frightened. At the time Daniel could not get Adanna out of the door, and the episode made him decide that he didn't want the children exposed to such behaviour. They had suffered enough.

When he got home that day he immediately phoned an estate agent and put the London house on the market. He knew of a good private school by the East Sussex coast which took children of diplomats and royals of all different nationalities, so he made enquiries there. The following weekend he drove them all down to the coast where, despite the coldness, they paddled in the water and made sandcastles and Daniel introduced them to ice cream. They stayed in a hotel for several days until he found a large detached house with a few acres of land in a small village.

Before he had gone to Africa, he had sold his share of his private surgery in London. This gave him almost enough money to pay for the new house outright. The rest he settled within weeks when he sold the house in Kensington. He tutored Adanna at home until the new school year started in September and then sent her to the private school as a day pupil. Jobi went to the village nursery.

Daniel no longer wanted to perform surgery, so he bought into a general practice and worked part time while Jobi was at nursery, fitting in visits to the hospital for Jobi's prosthetic hand. Now that Jobi had started on his second term of full days at the village primary school Daniel found he had too much time to himself, and his brooding got worse.

Heaving a sigh, he thought about Adanna. Now just turned fifteen, she had grown into a beautiful young lady. When she started school Daniel encouraged her to go out with friends, and at first she was invited to plenty of activities with her schoolmates, but she always refused so they soon stopped asking her. Her academic ability was beyond her years but socially she did not join in anything. She was still afraid to go out without Daniel and panicked if he was a little late collecting her from school. Then, six months ago, she had said that she no longer wanted to be a doctor because she would have to go away from Daniel to university. This was only resolved when Daniel pointed out that there was a good medical university in Brighton, only a half-hour drive from her school.

Adanna was still cleaning her teeth as many times a day as possible and showering obsessively, obviously because of the things she had been made to do with the commander and others. It was clear that these terrible memories were still uppermost in her mind and that she would not do anything or go anywhere without Daniel. Wrapping his dressing gown around his naked body and turning from the window, he thought that he really should look into some counselling for her straight away instead of putting it off and hoping she would suddenly be alright. After all, he had the whole day stretching in front of him once he had dropped the children off at school.

Resolved, he went downstairs to put the coffee on. Jobi came bursting into the kitchen with a big grin on his face, welly boots muddy and mud hanging from his school blazer, smearing dirt across the clean stone tiles. Daniel shook his head. He would have to sponge his blazer down before he took the kids to school. How many times had he told Jobi not to do things in his school uniform? Dirt seemed to jump onto him within seconds! However, Daniel could never be cross with Jobi – at least not for long – because he always looked too innocent and his eager pleasure and giggly nature were so enticing.

'Do you want egg on toast or egg and fingers?' Daniel asked, nearly spilling boiling water over Jobi from the coffee pot as Jobi discovered that wet boots slide wonderfully on tiles and slid to a stop just in front of him.

'Jobi!' Daniel shouted.

'Oops, sorry.'

'Egg ...'

'Please, with fingers.'

'Take your boots off and put them in the cupboard. They are making a mess on the floor. Mrs Jones has enough to do in your bedroom without more Jobi mayhem in the kitchen.'

'What's mayhem?'

'You,' said Daniel, smiling at Jobi's upturned face and luminous eyes that gleamed like a woodland river on a sunny day.

'My carrots are growing very big. I pulled one up and it was eeeeeeenormous! Then I buried it again so it can grow as big as this,' and he held his arms wide.

'Well, now you have pulled it up it will stop growing,' Adanna said, coming into the room. Her hair was immaculately braided and her uniform crisp. She looked as dainty as a flower as she slipped gracefully into her seat.

'No it won't, will it Dad?'

'Well, it might do, because you broke the roots, I expect. They need their roots to help make them grow.'

'Are they long stringy things?'

'Yes,' said Adanna.

'Oh, oh.' Jobi sat thinking for a moment. 'We will just have to have it for tea then. I'll go and get it.'

'No you will not, young man,' said Daniel, catching Jobi's arm with one hand as he balanced a plate in the other. 'Here is your egg. The carrot will be best left in the warm ground until you get home from school.'

'True,' said Adanna with a smile as Daniel arched his eyebrows at her.

Two days later Daniel went to meet the counsellor on his own. He had been told that she had an excellent reputation with war refugees but he wanted to meet her first. He needed to feel reassured that she understood Adanna's background completely.

'Mr Williams, you can go in now,' said the friendly receptionist as Daniel sifted uninterestedly through a magazine in the waiting room. He thanked her and entered a pale lavender room with soft, doughy beige settees and a fire crackling in the grate. It was not what Daniel expected. Neither was the dark-haired young woman looking up at him with soft blue eyes. Tendrils of hair had escaped the tight bun at the back of her head and cascaded around her oval face. Her sensual lips broke into a smile.

Odd sensations fluttered in Daniel's chest, making it hard for him to breathe. His legs felt wobbly. She was the most beautiful creature in the world, and the sweet smell of honeysuckle when she held out her well-manicured hand in greeting had his pulse doing the quickstep. When they actually touched hands he felt a rush of adrenaline that shot through his bloodstream and made his trousers tighten. Even the woman blinked as if she had had an electric shock.

'My name is Alicia Macey. Please sit down, Mr Williams. Coffee?'

'Ple—' Daniel swallowed hard to ease his bone-dry mouth. 'Please.'

'Milk and sugar?'

'Black, one sugar,' Daniel said hoarsely and sank into the luscious settee. It seemed to curl around his tense body. He watched Alicia bend over the coffee table as she poured the coffee. Her firm, round little bottom had him fantasising about her tight arse against him and arousal flew through his body like a runaway train. *My God,* he thought, *she would make a monk forget his vows!* He had been as celibate as a monk ever since he lost Shani. His whole reaction surprised him.

When she settled herself opposite him, her long slender legs crossed, Daniel had a hard time trying to concentrate on what she was saying and had to stare at a picture on the wall behind her until he managed to get a grip.

'Now, Mr Williams, I understand you wish to speak to me before I meet your daughter?'

'Yes,' Daniel cleared his throat. 'She is my adopted daughter.'

'Do you think that is the problem?'

'Oh no, her main problem is that she will not go anywhere except school without me.'

'And how long has this been going on for?'

'Well … Since I met her really. I was a doctor in Sierra Leone and she was a patient.'

'Why don't you start from the beginning?'

'I will.' Daniel paused and Alicia watched a shadow pass across his sable brown eyes, heavy with pain, and thought it was concern for the child. His empathy brought back memories of her gentle father and triggered a flare of heat as though she had been scorched. What was the matter with her? She had never reacted to men, which was why she was still a virgin. Then Alicia realised that she was having an episode of brain freeze; Daniel was talking again and here she was actually checking his assets out. She just did not do that!

'But what I want to know first,' Daniel was saying, 'is if you have had much experience with any children of war, or know much about how the children suffer from the horrific things they experience and see. Adanna is in a delicate state.'

A look of loneliness on Alicia's face struck Daniel like a blow. It was a minute before she answered.

'Twelve years ago I got mixed up in the former Yugoslav war for just under a year.'

'I'm sorry,' Daniel said quietly. 'You must have been very young.'

'Just fifteen, the age I believe your daughter is now. Tell me about Adanna.'

Chapter 8

All week Daniel alternated between feeling an inner glow and feeling guilty for finding Alicia so attractive ... No, overpowering with sensuality. He now found it easy to get out of bed and attack the day. His suffering seemed less intense and for the first time in two years he actually felt glad to be alive. It had been agreed that Adanna would see Alicia on her own; then, the following day – today – Daniel would also meet with Alicia to discuss the best way for him to help.

'Wow, you smell wonderful,' Adanna said, completely perplexed as she noted her papa's new shirt and smart appearance. This was a turn for the better, she thought. She wondered why.

'Thanks,' Daniel answered, and grinned.

Adanna's eyes fixed on his face. 'Maybe you could have a haircut next.'

Daniel raised his eyebrows in surprise. 'Do you think I need one, then?'

'Let's say you had a smooth bald head when we met and now your hair is nearly to your shoulders. You have never had it cut. You look like a hippy.'

'Yes, you make me have my hair cut!' Jobi joined in, scooping an over-laden spoon of Frosties into his mouth, half of which immediately dropped back into the bowl. Milk dribbled down his chin and hung for a moment with Daniel and Adanna staring at it, mesmerised. Too late, Daniel grabbed a section of kitchen roll and winced as a large globule of milk dropped onto Jobi's clean school shirt.

Adanna started giggling and Jobi smirked up at Daniel as he wet the paper and rubbed at Jobi's shirt, sighing.

'You are such a dirty little toad,' Daniel said, trying to sound stern. 'I think you should stay in the nude until it is nearly time for school.'

Jobi started laughing. 'What, show everyone my bum?'

'Oh no, please!' Adanna chuckled. 'He has only just started keeping his clothes on.'

'No, I haven't!' Jobi spat at Adanna. 'I never take them off in school.'

'You used to,' Adanna retorted.

'No I didn't, did I Dad?'

'When you were very small. Please finish your breakfast or we will be late for school.'

'What, when we were in Africa?'

'You never had any clothes on then.' Adanna shifted from the table and dropped her plate and spoon into the dishwasher. She hated talking or thinking about her homeland. Yesterday had been bad enough.

She had refused to talk when she first met Alicia until Alicia, with bright tears shining in her eyes, told her about her parents being murdered in front of her. Then Adanna had opened up and experienced her terrors all over again, including her ordeals with the commander. Up until then she had sometimes managed nearly a whole week without a bad dream, but last night she had been there again, vividly. She woke up with beads of perspiration dripping off her and thought for a moment that the commander was beside her in the dark. She switched on the light and looked around her room as if to confirm where she was. The dark dreams crumbled away like ashes but she was too frightened to close her eyes again; it had been too real.

Sitting up in bed with a large comfy cushion behind her she studied one of her medical books, the only thing she clung onto when her thoughts were distressing. She was to be a doctor, a doctor in this new land that was both unfamiliar and frightening. She had seen how some people gave her hostile glances and it brought a feeling of dread into her heart, reminding her of the hostility that she had endured from people she thought were her neighbours and friends in Africa. She could not trust anyone except her papa. He had shown how much he loved her by throwing her into the plane that day and taking her to this new world where people kept to themselves in strong brick houses.

A world where she saw the landscape turn white, as if God had waved a magic wand, making it dazzle in the winter sun like a mosaic carpet of molten jewels. A world where the trees dripped with glistening lacy leaves and star-shaped snowflakes gripped the edges of her bedroom window, and it was unbearably cold. Cold enough to hold her breath in the air when she spoke. Cold enough for her to need enough garments to keep a large family clothed in Africa. Then there was the rain; sweeping volleys of sharp arrows that rattled her bedroom windows. There were gusts of wind that made the willow tree dance with abandonment in the garden and sent the sea swirling, crashing, and threatening. However, she never missed her hot homeland, only her family. She was haunted by her three brothers. Were they still alive? What had happened to them? Some nights she thought she heard her younger brother calling her name and she would cuddle her pillow close, as if it was him, until she fell into a restless sleep.

Alicia looked radiant in a cornflower blue dress that emphasised her piercing blue eyes. It flattered her beautiful high-cheek boned face, neat little nose and full lips. Her raven hair was loose today, cascading around her shoulders, and Daniel wanted to run his hands through it and taste her lips.

Alicia, telling herself that Daniel was only a client's Father, had not been able to shift him from her mind and she had been out and bought a new dress; after all, she could do with some more 'work clothes'. As the scooped neckline left nothing to the imagination and the three-inch belt around her waist accentuated how tiny it was, the dress was not exactly suitable for work, but hell, why shouldn't she dress in whatever clothes she liked?

Feeling self-conscious, the pair went through the same formal ritual; a greeting, a tingling handshake, coffee. Daniel settled into the deep sofa and watched Alicia. Unguarded desire gushed through him and he had to grip the edge of the settee to keep himself from grabbing her. When she turned and bent over to hand him his coffee, her plump, soft breasts almost fell out of her dress. Daniel's heart banged in his throat as he imagined her nipples, swollen and hard, swaying into his open palms. He spilled the coffee as he took it. It made them both jump, brushing up against each other; they instantly sprang apart.

'Sorry – my fault,' Daniel said, standing upright, then quickly sitting down again to hide the erection in his trousers.

'I have some kitchen roll. I'll wipe you down and clear up the floor. No problem,' she said, her cheeks suddenly flaming as she glimpsed his bulge. 'Here.' She thought better of 'wiping him down' and handed him some kitchen paper.

Daniel had to look away, gazing at the painting hanging on the wall again, as Alicia crouched on the floor, her beautiful backside swaying as she cleaned. At this rate, Daniel thought, he would be able to paint the damn picture himself. He had never found any woman instantly sexy before – he had always had to get to know them before he got aroused, like with Shani and his wife and at university when he was younger. The sexual attraction this woman aroused in him had him nearly on the edge of losing his self-control. He put it down to his abstinence. It must be. No one could give off this amount of raw animal sexuality.

Alicia sat down with her arms folded firmly across her breasts as if she was protecting them from his thoughts. It caused them to dimple up in an erotic way which had Daniel breathing with difficulty, smiling helplessly like a schoolboy, trying to concentrate on what she was saying.

'Doctor Williams, is there a shop or a post office in your village not too far from your house?'

Surprised by her question he said, 'Yes, a Spar shop. Please call me Daniel, otherwise I shall feel like you are a patient.' He chuckled, laughter lines fanning out around his coffee brown eyes.

'Erm, Daniel, yes … erm, how far?'

'How far?'

'The shop from your house.'

'Oh, umm, about half a mile at the most.'

'Fine. Safe village, is it?'

'Well, yes; we only have about three roads, and about a hundred houses. There's a school, a pub and a church. It's more of a hamlet really. My house is at the back of the village green and the shop is down the road. Why?'

'Has Adanna ever been in the shop?'

'Sometimes we call in there for milk or something after I have picked her up from school.'

'Well, you need to give Adanna some responsibility by sending her on an errand to the shop, say for milk. You could conveniently run out on Saturday morning just before breakfast. Let her take her brother; that way she will not panic and come running back. She will feel that, because she is older, she must not show her fear. Encourage her and endorse the fact that she is quite capable and old enough – which she is.'

'I usually do the shopping on Saturday or run down to the shop if we run out of anything. Adanna will think it a bit unusual.'

'Be in your pyjamas and say you feel unwell if you feel you need to give her an excuse, although really she should help out. Give them money for sweets or ice cream as a treat for going.'

'Mmm.'

'Adanna told me about the dreadful things that happened to her, and what happened to Shani, her new Mother. But you are over-compensating and mollycoddling her; sort of disabling her.'

'I think that's wrong. I try to persuade her to do things. She just won't and I don't like to force it.'

'Why not?'

'Well, because I don't want her to be scared ever again.'

'But she is scared, scared of even her own shadow.'

'Yes, mmm, I see what you are saying. I never realised … looked at it like that. I thought she could not cope.'

'She can't if you don't let her. Start little, like the shop; not too much stress for the first time. She will do it and nothing will happen to her. That will give her confidence for the next time and bigger things.'

'OK, this Saturday it is, then.'

'I hope you don't mind me saying this, or take offence, but did you feel that what happened to Shani was your fault?'

Daniel stared, wide-eyed; then his lips tightened and he said quietly, 'It was. I should have thrown Shani into the helicopter like the children, then got aboard myself, instead of thinking I could make space for her from inside the helicopter. They said there was no room. I should have been the one left behind.'

'You cannot think like that. It was not your fault. These things happen. It is no good saying "what if". That is why you are over-protecting Adanna. You think you let Shani down and you are determined not to let Adanna down.'

'Yes.'

'The best way to protect Adanna and Jobi is to make them independent and give them coping skills. Maybe even self-defence classes would be good.'

Daniel looked deeply into Alicia's eyes and his insides shook with desire. He could drown in those eyes, those warm swirls of blue like a mountain stream; maybe he had already drowned. Before he could stop himself the torment about his wife came tumbling out. 'It is not the first time I have let people down and it has ended in their death.'

Alicia stretched out her fingers and clasped Daniel's hand. Sparks flew between them and Daniel quickly removed his hand. He wished he had not told her. He had never told anyone, not even his parents.

'Tell me,' Alicia whispered. Her breath seemed to curl around him like an angel's kiss.

His guard collapsed. 'I killed my wife and son,' he said, his voice cracked with distress.

'How?'

'Because I was too stubborn as usual. I was tired and had had a couple of glasses of wine.'

'And?'

'I had worked in surgery until the early hours, then, after only a couple of hours of sleep, we went to a family party. It was held in the garden and because it started to rain, the party broke up. Some people stayed but I wanted to go home, which we did. My wife asked to drive, but I insisted I would, because by then the rain had become heavy. We were nearly home when this car swerved and came rushing towards us on the wrong side of the road. The next thing I knew I was waking up in hospital. Catherine was dead and Reece was in a coma. I only had a broken elbow. Reece lived for two more days. I prayed and prayed, but he died, never regaining consciousness.'

This time Alicia moved to Daniel's side and wrapped him in her arms, holding him as he broke down sobbing, his first release since it had happened. The grief smashed the strength from his limbs and he sagged, resting his head on her silky breasts while she soothed him like a child.

Chapter 9

The next day Daniel did not have to pretend to feel ill; his head thumped and his body ached like he had the flu. The night before, just before he went to bed, he remembered to pour the remains of the milk down the sink, which was just as well as it took him a while to drag himself out of bed and the children were up watching TV before him.

'We haven't had any breakfast. We are out of milk,' Jobi greeted him.

'Oh.'

'Shall we have breakfast out? We are both dressed,' said Adanna, grinning at her father's dishevelled state.

'No, I don't feel well. If I give you some money you and Jobi can go to the village shop and get some milk.'

Alarm flashed across Adanna's features like a shaft of sunlight across a quiet landscape. She opened her mouth to protest, but Jobi was jumping up and down, eager-hearted, already contemplating the adventure.

Daniel turned away from Adanna's terrified face and strode to the kitchen counter seeking his wallet. Not meeting her stricken eyes, he said casually, 'One pint of milk and buy yourself both some sweets,' and handed her some money.

Jobi screeched with excitement, rushed into the hall, found his shoes and shoved them on without being told.

Daniel, holding his head, said, 'Stop screaming, Jobi. You are only going down the road, not to the other side of the moon. Hold Adanna's hand and do as she tells you. No nonsense.'

'Can't you drive down there?' Adanna asked.

'No, Adanna, I don't feel good. You will be OK, the shop is practically next door. Put your jackets on,' and Daniel turned swiftly from the hall and went into the kitchen. He felt sick.

As soon as he heard the door slam he raced to the upstairs window and watched them go down the road. Adanna hesitated at the gate until Jobi yanked her hand, jabbering and practically dancing along the road. When a car raced past, Adanna's head shot round as though it was an enemy tank. She halted again and swung around to look back at the house. Daniel held his breath. However, Jobi said something and she started walking again. Alicia was right, he thought, and watched until they were out of sight.

Slowly Daniel came down the stairs. To distract himself from worrying about Adanna he started emptying the dishwasher and thought about his disgraceful behaviour in front of Alicia the day before. It filled him with hot shame. He had cried like a child for nearly half an hour. He had broken down completely while she sensitively coaxed out his emotions in a matter-of-fact way until he was empty. All desire for her had vanished like a dream, although he had noticed how his tears had dribbled onto her breasts and glistened on her smooth skin. The thought now had Daniel as stiff as a rod, but how could he ever look her in the eye again?

He stared out of the window as he idly washed up the dirty glasses he never put in the dishwasher, watching the sun sprinkle its rays onto the leaves of the willow tree, making them glisten as the branches swayed like long arms of a green monster in the breeze. He gave a deep, long sigh; he did feel cleansed, his heart lighter and at peace, for the first time since the loss of his four-year-old son. A life hardly started.

It was nearly half an hour since the children had left for the shop, a five-minute walk at the most, and Daniel began to worry. He hurried up the stairs two at a time to look out of the upstairs window, his heart beating double time as morbid imagination took over. A sun-bright smile slowed his heart as he saw Adanna and Jobi, no longer holding hands, chatting and ambling along the street like any other kids. Feeling warm inside, he practically skipped to the kitchen and started reaching for bowls and cereals.

Chapter 10

Alicia lay in bed, staring up at the ceiling. She was naked under the sheet. She felt like a different woman; no, she felt like a woman for the first time now that she was falling in love. Was it love? Love, love, love … She had thought it could never happen to her. She thought love had left her soul a long time ago. She hardly thought about or even looked at men. Why did she find Daniel so different?

Yesterday had been an emptying of held-back emotions for them both, although Daniel had been unaware of it just like he was unaware of her. But for the first time she wanted a man! She found Daniel's gentle and caring nature such a turn-on; she saw the likeness of his nature to that of her father and brother. Men who would never hurt a woman and a doctor who would never hurt anybody. She had known a doctor that would; she had seen his evil and touched it. Daniel was a wonderful, loving doctor; a person who saved lives, not took them. How she hoped she had convinced him of that.

She stretched her slim body under the sheet and swept her hands down her torso. Daniel oozed sexuality and she wondered what it would be like to make love to him. Her hormones made her crave his body as her visions came with his smell, tantalising her and making her skin prickle. She began fantasising about his kisses and felt the same hot glow in her belly as she had the previous day when she held him against her as his body shook with heart-breaking sobs. She had wanted him to stay there; that was hardly professional!

He had soon pushed himself away and, although he continued to cry as she asked him questions, he got himself under control at last. She tittered to herself at the memory of him wiping his tears and nose on his shirt sleeve like a schoolboy. He had looked at her and apologised with a grin which, if he had only known it, had practically melted her into a puddle at his feet.

Alicia slipped her shapely legs over the side of the bed, placing her feet onto the cold wooden floor. She padded to the bathroom, where she stepped under the needle-sharp spray of the shower, letting it run rivers over her naked body. She needed to get her mind in order and go food shopping, to stop thinking about a man who would probably never give her a second thought – especially if he knew what she was capable of, her murderous past. Then promptly her traitorous body ached with need for him. Was this lust or love, this longing, living in a half world where you could not train your thoughts? Heck, it was hell … No, hell was the dreams, the flashbacks.

She realised that for the first time since her family had been killed she had not had the dream last night – the dream that kept her from living, kept her from seeking pleasure. Instead she had dreamt about Daniel. Amazed at herself, she towel-dried her body and, still naked in front of the oval bathroom mirror, stood brushing her thick hair until it shone. Grimacing, she thought it resembled a lion's mane except for the colour. *I wonder what sort of hair Daniel likes. Maybe black. The African woman Shani must have had black hair, but probably not as much as I've got … I wonder what his wife Catherine was like; dark or blonde? Oh, please ... think about what shopping you need.*

The images of Daniel persisted even in the supermarket, and it took her forever to finish her shopping. As she picked out some vegetables she wondered what food he liked; when she reached for shampoo she wondered if his hair felt soft; when she sniffed the soaps she became aware that she was randomly picking them up to try and find his smell. Annoyed with herself, her insides wobbly, she grabbed her usual soap. Even putting her goods away into the cupboards had her thinking about what sort of house he lived in, if he was a neat and tidy person or a relaxed, muddled person.

She smiled at the memory of her dad telling her, after she had made cakes in the kitchen that she was organised chaos and that the kitchen resembled a war zone. He had asked her if she had won the battle. Nevertheless, no war had been like the mess she had made that day. She had a brief flashback of her half-burnt house, black and charred like her parents and ... the baby. She would not go there. Not today, when only a minute ago she had felt so happy. Why did her thoughts have to return to the scars in her heart?

With tears blurring her vision she glanced around for her car keys. Finding them, she clasped them and, grabbing her jacket, slipped out of the house and drove for ten minutes to the coast. Not for the first time she thought about buying a dog. Her walks along the beach were lonely, but the smell and the soft sand under her feet always blew the haunting cobwebs away.

Strolling along the edge of the water, the ripples cold against her bare toes, listening to the overhead screeching of the gulls, she thought how good it would be for Adanna to get a dog. She could be responsible for walking it each day; there must be some nice walks near where they lived.

Resolved to find out exactly where Daniel did live, Alicia found herself driving past his house half hour later. My goodness – was she stalking him? No; that was what she had done to the Zerac family after *he* had murdered her family. The entire Zerac family had used the cover of the war for their malicious sick business, but she had stopped that.

Daniel's house was not what Alicia expected. It looked like a chocolate box house, set back from the village green, with the most stunning pale lavender roses rambling over the front wall of the house. The drive was a semicircle of cobbled stone running between two gates about fifty yards apart so that you could drive through without turning. Underneath the two front windows grew a romantic cottage garden with wallflowers, poppies, lupins foxgloves and blue delphiniums, their statuesque spires as tall as flags and their reflections bouncing off the dark windows behind. A spiked black iron fence ran the length of the plot between the two wrought iron gates and a rose garden peeped out from the edge of the cobbled driveway. Alicia could smell the strong scent of the roses from her car.

Beside the arched porch were two statues of fairies holding baskets from which multi-coloured lobelia flowers dripped. Several pots alongside held a sea of upturned pansy faces. It was obvious that the garden was loved and that it was important to the people who lived there. Alicia wondered if Daniel had a gardener or if he did the garden himself. She enjoyed gardening; she liked the physical exertion of the job and the satisfied feeling at the end – although gardening was never finished. That was another thing she liked about gardens; they continued to grow even when neglected.

Alicia toured the village, noting the small stone church, the antique pub, the primary and junior schools and, just outside the village, a small wood and a river, all as picturesque as Daniel's garden. The forest made her shiver; she never walked in a wood anymore, preferring the open fields or the shore. As a child she had loved to stroll amongst the trees, she and her family walking for miles most weekends. She used to throw sticks for their old dog Kipper and climb trees with her brother, which scared her mother and made her father laugh and encourage them both to clamber higher. She was very skilled at climbing trees. That was how she had hidden and escaped that awful night.

Coldness swept over Alicia, a coldness so deep that she shut down. She felt no emotion as she drove out of the village and headed for home. She didn't see the flowering hedgerows or the beauty of the countryside that surrounded her, and a tear like silver glistened in the corner of her eye. Suddenly she couldn't wait to be home, where she could tumble into bed, curl up like a cat and hide in the dark under the bedclothes until the shadowy sense of fear that was overwhelming her would leave her body drained and limp.

Chapter 11

It was after the next counselling session that Daniel contrived to get Alicia to come out with him and the children at the weekend. He had agreed to get a dog and was delighted at Adanna's excited reaction to the idea. She was even more excited than Jobi.

Daniel had never owned a dog, so, as Alicia had, he asked her to come with them and help choose one. They picked an adorable King Charles spaniel, grey with black splashes, droopy ears, big eyes and such a cute expression that they were all unable to resist him – although the dog actually chose them! As soon as they arrived at the kennels he threw himself at Adanna's legs. She bent down and lifted him up. His soft furry body wriggled with pleasure and he licked her face. They named him Squirt as he was no bigger than Daniel's hand and was the 'runt' of the litter. He had been vaccinated and toilet trained and was ready to be taken home.

There was an argument between the two children about who should hold him in the back of the car, so Daniel decided that Alicia should have him on her lap until they bought a cage at a nearby shop. Daniel ended up buying not only a cage but also a lead, dog food, treats, a blanket and a fluffy hot water bottle!

'What on earth does he want a hot water bottle for?' asked Daniel. 'He will be living inside the house!'

'Because he will probably miss his mum and will want something to snuggle up against, at least for several nights,' said Alicia, which led to the children pleading for Squirt to be allowed to sleep on their bed.

As Alicia gathered up various dog toys to stop Squirt from biting the furniture, Daniel wondered if he had bitten off more than he could chew, buying a dog. *More than I can chew – very funny!* He shook his head and, sighing, popped the toys into the basket. Next, the children and Alicia decided that the dog should be taken for a walk, so they had to buy poo bags and a scoop.

'Poo bags!' Daniel exclaimed shrilly, and Alicia turned and gave him 'the look.'

The sea was as bright as a diamond in the sun as they strolled along the shore, Squirt barking at the waves and backtracking away from them. The two children's laughter rang out after him and Adanna tried to coax him into the shallow water to paddle with her, telling him there was nothing to be afraid of.

Daniel raised his eyebrows at Adanna's words and glanced at Alicia, who flashed him her warm smile. A churning of longing started in the pit of his stomach. Throwing a blanket over the sand, Daniel and Alicia settled down to watch the children. Adanna began throwing a ball across the beach for Squirt to chase, but he just yapped at it and Adanna found herself racing over and retrieving the ball time and time again. Eventually, fed up, Squirt trotted over to Jobi.

Jobi had started digging a hole and Squirt began to nose the mound of sand that Jobi was piling up at the side, making Squirt sneeze and shake his head. He shook his head so fiercely at one point that he fell into the hole, which was filled with sea water. He yelped in fear and scrambled out, whimpering, his fur bedraggled. Adanna picked him up, nursing him.

'You should watch what you're doing Jobi, you have frightened him. There, there, Squirt, I've got you.'

'It was not my fault. He started messing with my sand pile. Is he alright?'

Daniel grinned to himself and turned to Alicia. 'You are clever! Adanna is obviously going to be Squirt's protector.'

'Yes, looks like it, and in teaching him not to be frightened she will overcome some of her own fear.'

'Err, would you like to come back home for dinner with us later?' Daniel had been toying with the idea from the start.

'Love to, but I'm a vegetarian. Since the war and the death of my family, I can't eat meat. I won't tell you what it reminds me of.'

Daniel took Alicia's hand. He had wanted to touch her ever since he set eyes on her, and had been clinging onto his wits each time she was near, but this was a gesture to show that he understood, so he just squeezed her slender hand gently. She did not need to go into detail; it was similar to why he could no longer perform surgery since he had come back from Sierra Leone.

'That's fine. Do you eat cheese? I could make a macaroni cheese pasta; we all like that. Do you want to tell me about your family?'

Alicia shook her head. 'I haven't got any. They all died. Maybe one day.'

Chapter 12

The evening passed far too quickly for Alicia, although it was nearly midnight when she left Daniel's house. Once the children had gone to bed – with a kiss each for Alicia, much to her astonishment – she and Daniel settled down with glasses of wine. They laughed together about the day's events, and when Squirt jumped up onto Daniel's lap he cuddled him as if it was an everyday occurrence.

'That will become a habit, climbing onto laps, unless you stop it right now,' said Alicia.

'Mmm, I expect the kids will let him do it, so no hassle.'

'What about when he comes in all muddy and you all have clean clothes on, or the children have their school uniforms on?'

Daniel smirked. 'You're right. I have enough trouble keeping Jobi clean as it is.'

'Let's put him in his bed and tuck him in with the hot water bottle.'

Daniel boiled the kettle and poured it into the furry hot water bottle. Squirt fell fast asleep in his bed within seconds, and Daniel hoped he would stay that way until morning. He didn't fancy a night of whining.

They settled once more on the cushioned sofa, this time with glasses of hot chocolate accompanied by cream and marshmallows. Alicia giggled and Daniel raised his eyebrows questioningly.

'Yes?'

'Nothing. I'm just not used to such luxurious hot chocolate.'

'Oh, it's not luxurious in our house; the kids only drink it this way.'

They sat and talked, but kept the conversation light, as they were so aware of each other. Alicia thought that Daniel oozed magnetic sex appeal, and he kept giving her sleepy, sexy looks that could practically make her clothes drop off. They spoke about their gardens and plants, which they both loved, and how they liked going for long walks and bike rides. It was nice to have so much in common. Then, just before Alicia left, as they stood at the front door and she fumbled in her bag for her car keys, Daniel surprised her by suggesting that they go out on a date as soon as he could arrange childcare.

'Which evening would be best for you?' asked Daniel, when Alicia accepted.

'Oh, most evenings except Wednesdays. I go bowling with two friends from work.'

Daniel stepped towards Alicia and gave her a lingering goodnight kiss. For a deliciously long moment she stayed pressed up against him, his heart started thundering and his senses reeling from the taste of her as he slowly let her go and helped her on with her jacket.

Still feeling the gentle touch of Daniel's lips on hers, Alicia practically skipped to the car. It was the most wonderful evening she had had since before her grandfather died when she was eighteen – no, longer; since she was a child. The laughter, the cosiness and the love that had flowed around the house that evening brought back good memories of her own family and she wished she could become part of this one, but she knew that this was only fantasy.

A warm feeling flooded her body and she tossed her head to dismiss it. Inside she knew that she was not right for any family. She had dark thoughts and was capable of killing as easily as any assassin. She had made a vow to herself over the grave of her dead brother and sister-in-law and promised them that she would see all their murderers' dead. That vow had been only partly executed.

Yes, she had killed all the men and the whole Zerac family when she found out that they all indulged in the same vile practice, but she had not got him – Doctor Petrov Zerac himself. The one contact she had followed to his home town had disappeared without a trace. If only she had not been in the hospital for so long, but the wound on her head and her exhausted condition had kept her there for a week. She had pretended that she did not know who she was and had lost her memory; all the time she was frightened that he might turn up at her bedside, one of the constant flow of doctors.

After a week she left the hospital one night as swiftly and silently as she had arrived. She made a camp under a bridge opposite the Zerac house and waited. It was three days before she discovered what the Zeracs were up to. There was no sign of Petrov Zerac, so she followed his father one day, hoping he might lead her to his son. Unfortunately, he only led her to a warehouse where, later that night, she discovered the neatly wrapped boxes. She knew, then, that she would kill them all, even if it meant her own death too.

Later she trailed the mother and daughter to a large, grey-bricked house of horror and was so repelled by what she saw that she nearly passed out. The following evening she saw Petrov's older brother visit the warehouse with his uncle. That night she raided the local fighting group's ammunition stores and took a semi-automatic assault weapon.

She waited until she saw the whole Zerac family come home for dinner the next evening, then aimed the assault weapon and blew them all to smithereens. Afterwards she released the woman from the house of horror and blew that to bits too. Lastly she moved on to the warehouse, where she took all the money in the safe and gave most of it to the woman. Together they carried all the tiny boxes to the nearby cemetery and buried them before she demolished the warehouse.

Another week passed before she was able to confirm that she had killed all of the Zeracs except Petrov. She hung about for the funeral thinking that he would surely come, but he didn't. After another few days she bought a ticket to England with the money she had kept from the safe.

That night in bed Alicia settled to sleep thinking of Daniel, but the shooting of her parents and the killing of her brother and sister-in-law woke her up. She was covered in beads of perspiration. She made her way slowly down the stairs and fetched herself a drink, then sat watching the sun come up and thinking about her date with Daniel. It was the first date she had ever been on. She had had plenty of offers but she always refused them. What was it about Daniel that had made her say yes, even though she knew she was starting something that could not go anywhere? She was far from suitable for a gentle man like Daniel.

It was lunacy and pure lust, she told herself. She was so aware of him physically that it made her quite giddy. She was usually afraid of physical contact with men and kept her distance, which she had never found difficult before. What she had witnessed with the Zerac family during the war had seen to that.

She tried to tell herself that not all men were like them; her father and brother for instance … and her kindly grandfather … and now Daniel. She tried to analyse it. Was she looking for a father figure? Daniel was like her father in nature and looks. Dark hair and liquid brown eyes. The vision gave her goose bumps. He was older than her by just under eight years; hardly a father figure. And he had the most marvellous torso. No big muscles, just hard pecs – weren't they called that? When they were sitting on the beach he had taken off his tee-shirt. A shiver had shot down Alicia's spine and he had noticed and grinned. She found herself blushing even now at the thought. With a sigh she picked up her cup and wandered into the kitchen. It was time to shower and meet the day.

Halfway through Alicia's breakfast the phone rang. It was Adanna. 'Papa said will you come with us to the park and help train Squirt to behave himself on the lead?' Adanna giggled. 'We tried him in the garden, but he refuses to walk. He just sits on his bum and we have to pull him along.'

In the background Alicia heard Daniel shout, 'Say "please", Adanna, and only if it is convenient.'

Alicia's heart beat double time; she had wondered what to do and Sunday had seemed so long, stretching in front of her, until this moment. She arranged to meet them at the park in an hour. As soon as she put the phone down she raced upstairs to change out of her old jeans and tee-shirt into a pair of turquoise three-quarter length trousers and a low-cut black top. She found some dangly jet earrings and piled her hair on top of her head, where she clipped it with a big ebony hairclip. She shaded her eyelids with a light dusting of pale blue to emphasise the colour of her eyes, then swept mascara across her lashes and finished the look with some apricot lipstick.

Back down in the kitchen she tipped the remains of her cereal into the bin and decided to make a picnic. She gathered half a dozen eggs, put them in a saucepan to boil and started making a salad. She cut up some cheese and rummaged in the cupboard for fruit. On the way to the park she would stop and buy juice, a bottle of fizz and some wine, she thought. She pulled down her picnic basket and filled it with the food she had prepared, then added some serviettes and condiments. Yes, that was it, she told herself.

Then she remembered the picnic blanket. Where was it? She could not recall the last time she had used it. Hurrying upstairs, she searched the cupboards and drawers and eventually found it. It was in the spare bedroom, stuffed inside her grandfather's old music box stool that she never used any more. All the time she was trembling inside.

Chapter 13

Daniel slept like a log after Alicia left. If Squirt whined he didn't hear him, and he was amazed when he looked at the clock and saw that it was nearly nine already. The taste of Alicia and the feeling of her slender body against him came floating into his brain, which turned to mash when he thought about it.

When Daniel pulled the curtains, the children were in the garden trying to get Squirt to walk up the path with his lead on. Adanna was coaxing him with a biscuit some distance away, while Jobi held his lead and was tugging him towards Adanna. However, the pup sat solidly on his bottom. Daniel laughed out loud at their antics and, still chuckling, went down to the kitchen. As he drunk his coffee he thought about Alicia, her lovely face and little plump breasts and such long legs … Oh, how he had wanted to kiss her all over! The thought had him as stiff as a poker and he picked up his mobile and texted Mrs Jones to ask if she could babysit sometime this week. Then he strolled out to the garden and leant against the tree, watching the children with Squirt.

'He won't walk on his lead,' cried Jobi.

'Well, maybe it is too tight around his neck,' said Daniel, thinking with alarm that they might be accidentally strangling the dog. He leapt over to the pup. Squirt looked pleased to see him and wagged his tail, nearly falling over with excitement.

'We had it looser,' said Adanna, 'but then he just slips his head out of it and runs around the garden with us chasing him.'

'Yes, we had a hard job catching him again too,' protested Jobi. 'How do you get a dog to walk on a lead?'

Daniel shook his head. 'I'm not sure. You will have to ask Alicia.'

'Oh, OK, I'll phone her. We wanted to take Squirt to the park; can Alicia come too?'

Daniel had been racking his brains for an excuse to see Alicia today on a Sunday or before Adanna's next counselling session on Tuesday.

The day was already warm and the trees around the car park glistened like gold. When Daniel jumped out of the car and turned to open the door for Jobi, who had Squirt on a lead and was trying to pull him out, he saw Alicia coming towards them. She walked as delicately as a nymph and her face erupted in a luminous smile when she saw that he had seen her. God, she was gorgeous, thought Daniel, and again had trouble with tight jeans. Just then Squirt yelped and Daniel somehow managed to tear his eyes away from Alicia to see poor Squirt struggling between the two children as they fought to get him out of the car.

'I'll do it,' said Daniel, grabbing hold of Squirt and his lead and lifting him out of the car to the ground, where he promptly sat on his bottom. Daniel dropped the lead to lock the car. Suddenly Squirt spotted Alicia and rushed over to her, his lead trailing behind him, throwing himself at her feet as if asking for mercy – probably from the children, thought Daniel.

'I have brought a picnic in return for your dinner last night.'

'Wow, I love picnics,' cried Jobi, and took Alicia's hand. First surprise and then other emotions swept across her features when she gazed down at Jobi. It stirred the depths of Daniel's insides and he gulped, wanting to cry; he could see that she was starved of love, family love, because all her family were dead. How he wanted to wrap his arms around her and hold her close! And he might have done, but she had already recovered and was walking off with Jobi and Adanna, who had picked up Squirt. They were both listening intently to the instructions she was giving them about walking with Squirt. Daniel caught them up and relieved Alicia of the picnic basket. It was surprisingly heavy.

Adanna put Squirt down on the grass. She held his lead and looked ahead, not down at him. Jobi, Daniel and Alicia continued to walk on while Squirt sat on his bottom. Adanna patted the side of her leg, just like Alicia had instructed her to do, and Squirt looked up at her, but still she looked ahead. She took several small steps and patted the side of her leg again.

The rest of the family were now about a hundred yards in front and Daniel was worried about Adanna. Being away from his side in an open space was not normal for her, and he glanced quickly behind him. Adanna grinned and patted her leg again, taking another few steps. Daniel sighed with relief. She was more concerned with Squirt then about staying next to him.

They were half way across the park and heading for the lake before Squirt, with Adanna running alongside, came bounding up to them. They all made a fuss of him and gave him a treat. Then it was Jobi's turn. This time they were only a few hundred yards away when Squirt caught them up. Soon they were all strolling around the lake together, with Squirt sniffing out interesting places and Jobi allowing him to do so, until they found a patch of thick grass. Daniel spread the check blanket out and they all sat down on it. Squirt, no longer on his lead, took up most of the room, rolling about on his back with his soft pink belly exposed until Adanna, laughing, rubbed his tummy and he squirmed with pleasure.

Daniel and Alicia gazed at the muddy-coloured lake in front of them. Nestled in the sandy shore were reeds and bushes along with discarded feathers and floating dead leaves into which ducks, geese and swans were plunging their beaks hoping to find food. Sometimes a passing child would throw some stale bread at them, their shrill squawks and flapping wings creating a noisy squabble until the bread was eaten. Then they would glide serenely away. Usually Jobi would throw some bread, but today he was far too interested in Squirt, who was now sitting with Adanna watching children and adults playing on the grass. Several big dogs came up to say hallo, but Squirt dived behind Adanna and Jobi shooed them off. Then the children decided to get Squirt's ball out, but he still had no idea how to fetch it, and besides, he preferred being chased by the children.

Daniel and Alicia sat together, watching.

'Oh, this is lovely,' said Alicia, sipping a glass of wine.

'Mmm,' cooed Daniel, lying across the blanket and leaning on one arm, gazing at Alicia. Lovely she certainly was. Tendrils of hair had stuck to the graceful lines of her neck. Her neck was so kissable! His groin tightened as he watched her sensual lips kiss the glass she was drinking from.

His slow, suggestive smile made Alicia's nipples harden and she took another quick sip of her wine. As if she could read his thoughts, she smiled back foolishly and met his gaze for a beat. As he took her hand a little frisson of lust zinged through both of their bodies. His thumb stroked the back of her hand and she tensed as heat rocketed up to her throat.

'I've arranged for Mrs Jones, my home help, to have the kids on Friday night; is that OK?'

Alicia nodded. She was finding it hard to act normally, and he was only holding her hand! Oh hell …

'I thought we might go to dinner at Alfonso's. They have a large veggie selection and do lots of pasta too.'

'That sounds good. I've heard a lot of good comments about that restaurant.'

'Yes; I like it. What time shall I pick you up? And I need your address. Do you work late on Fridays?'

'No. Technically I don't work at all on Fridays, unless I arrange a session because my clients cannot make any other time.'

Daniel flashed his lopsided grin and Alicia's heart did a flip. 'Oh, great,' he said. 'I don't have surgeries on Fridays either. I only do three days a week. Monday, Wednesday and Thursday.'

'I work each morning Monday, Tuesday and Thursday and all day Wednesday.'

Immediately, thoughts of afternoons and days together without the kids shot into Daniel's mind. He felt a twinge of guilt for thinking about enjoying time without them. Still, he did need some grown up company too, he reasoned. His gaze fell upon Alicia's breasts, which were pressing hard against her top, looking as if they were about to pop out completely. She moved to a more comfortable position and pulled her hand away from his.

She had to move; Daniel was so close that she could see her reflection in his eyes and smell the male scent of his aftershave. The memory of last night's kiss was so overwhelming that for a moment she thought she might kiss him!

'Let's go and play ball with the children. After all, it is their day,' said Alicia, jumping up. She could no longer relax next to Daniel.

Daniel sighed and picked up the large plastic football that was sitting on the grass next to the picnic basket. He yelled at the kids and, out of frustration, kicked the ball harder than he had meant to. One minute, he thought, she seemed to like him, then the next ... Jobi went racing over to get the ball.

Daniel's thoughts went round and round as if caught in a maze. Was Alicia playing hard to get or was she really that shy? Or was she frightened because of ... What? He stood watching her laugh with the children. She scooped Jobi

up and wrestled with him for the ball he was cuddling.
Squirt, not wanting to be left out, was yapping at their legs.
No, Daniel thought, she was not playing with him, so that
only left the alternative – something horrific had happened
to her. He felt himself flush with anger, just as he had over
Adanna and her treatment when he had first met her. He
stared across the grass towards Adanna. She appeared like
any other young girl having fun, giggling and chasing Alicia,
who had the ball. No one could see the tormented scarring of
her mind.

Adanna and Alicia had been together for well over an hour
when Daniel came to pick Adanna up from her Tuesday
session. To his surprise they both came out laughing like two
secretive schoolgirls. Alicia, wearing a brightly coloured
floral dress that seemed to float around her slim frame as she
walked, aroused the usual response in Daniel's body.

'Alicia has finished for today and she is going to take
me – and you, if you're good – to the homemade burger bar
and then, if you give me permission and some money, she
will take me shopping. I could do with some new clothes.'

Daniel stood with his mouth open like a goldfish. He
was so amazed. Adanna going somewhere without him and
actually shopping for clothes!

'I can drop her at your house when we've finished,'
said Alicia, looking at Daniel's stupefied expression.

'Er, mmm, yes, of course, that will be fine,' he
answered, coming back to life. 'Where's this burger bar
then? I thought you didn't eat meat.'

'It's around the corner, on the corner of Jackson's in the precinct. They do veggieburgers with cheese, salad and chips, and I'm starving, so race you there.' And with that Alicia broke into a sprint, Adanna and Daniel running after her. Daniel had noticed how fast she could run on Sunday in the park. He had also noticed her long and shapely legs.

It was six-thirty when the girls came back from shopping. Daniel and Jobi were reading together when they tumbled through the door, dropping several boxes and bags because they were carrying too much … or had bought too much! Daniel raised his eyebrows at the pile on the floor and Adanna giggled at his expression as she placed the remaining bags on the settee.

'You left anything in the shops?' grinned Jobi, voicing what Daniel had been thinking.

'Oh, don't be silly, of course, and somewhere among the bags there's something for you and Dad too.'

'Oh, cool,' Jobi said, jumping up and shoving the book at Daniel.

'You look as if you could do with a cuppa.' Daniel smiled up at Alicia. 'Bet it was harder work then you thought.'

Alicia smiled. 'Shopping for fun is not hard work. It was great. I haven't been shopping with another female since I was little, with my mum. But I could certainly do with a cup of tea.'

Daniel nodded. He wandered into the kitchen and put the kettle on. Alicia trailed after him just as Jobi gave a squeal of pleasure. He had found his present.

Daniel grabbed two cups and placed them on saucers. 'What did you buy Jobi?'

Before Alicia could answer, Jobi came racing into the kitchen hauling a large Scooby- Doo.

'Look what Adanna bought me! Isn't he big?' The soft furry dog was nearly as big as Jobi. It took all Daniel's self-control to stop himself from laughing out loud, because Jobi was squeezing Scooby-Doo and Jobi's eyes looked as big as gobstoppers in his small face next to Scooby-Doo's large head and scrunched-up face.

Then Squirt spotted the toy and started barking and going for Scooby-Doo's leg. Jobi shouted at Squirt; Squirt backed off, barking, then jumped at the toy and knocked Jobi over. Both Daniel and Alicia, seeing what was about to happen, rushed to grab Squirt. They bumped heads and Alicia fell over Jobi as she bent to grasp him. She staggered backwards, putting her hand out to break her fall. Daniel managed to scoop up Squirt and chucked him out of the back door into the garden, where he proceeded to bark and run around.

Turning, he saw Alicia sitting on the kitchen floor nursing her hand, which was rapidly turning mauve. Adanna, who had been standing in the kitchen doorway, took a clean tea towel from a drawer and dislodged some ice cubes from the ice dispenser into it. Luckily Jobi had landed on Scooby-Doo so he was unhurt. Daniel lifted Alicia up and carried her gently into the sitting room, where he planted her on the settee.

'It's my hand that hurts, not my legs,' Alicia protested as she was swept into close contact with Daniel's chest and engulfed in his arms. But she didn't move, his male aroma swishing like a powerful wave in her brain. When he smiled into her eyes, she suddenly felt just like jelly … but it was from surprise, she told herself.

Daniel took Alicia's hurt hand and moved her wrist about, checking to see if she had broken it. She winced. 'See if you can move your wrist yourself, please.' Satisfied that Alicia had not broken her wrist, Daniel took the cold tea towel from Adanna and wound it around Alicia's hand, praising Adanna for her knowledge and quick thinking.

'Sorry,' Jobi said, coming over and sinking down next to Alicia.

'There is no need to say sorry. It was an accident, not your fault.'

'I'll make that tea,' said Daniel. 'Stay put, and as you are a bit shocked I think you should stay the night. I don't like you being left on your own; shock can linger. We have a spare bedroom.' And he grinned to himself as he heard the children pleading with Alicia to stay.

She didn't stand a chance!

'It's lucky you are right-handed, but I doubt if you will be able to go bowling tomorrow night,' said Daniel, coming back from the kitchen carrying two teas.

Alicia sniggered inwardly at Daniel's concern. Shock! This wasn't 'in shock'. Shock was when you saw your parents shot dead and when your brother had been tortured and died in your arms and his wife cut open and raped. However, she wasn't going to enlighten him or argue because she just loved to stay in this warm family environment.

When Daniel placed the tea beside Alicia he saw her frozen eyes and a Morse code of memories crossing her face. Coldness swept his skin and he felt as though his soul had been sucked out of him. He put his hand gently over her uninjured hand and she looked unseeingly into his face. Then, as if a cloud had moved to allow the sun to peep through again, she smiled softly, mystically. Seeing her sunny smile, he knew that the bad memories had faded. He was determined to find out what had happened in her life that was so dreadful she could not even talk about it.

Alicia was glad she had hurt her hand. She adored the laughter that she shared with the children and Daniel. After he had bandaged Alicia's hand, Adanna had shown her father the clothes she had bought. Alicia and the children were in stitches at his reactions. To Alicia's astonishment, Daniel had quite old-fashioned views on what Adanna should wear. He didn't like many of the items, although he tried to hide his disapproval from Adanna when she frowned at him. He thought a couple of the skirts were too short, several tops too revealing and a dress too old for her. None of them were. The skirts were short, but just above the knee – longer than most youngsters wore. The tops were laughably ordinary and revealed no skin or breast, but were clingy and showed off her developing figure. The dress was just right for the summer school dance for which it was intended. It was made of pale peach chiffon, gathered softly at the waist, with a slightly scooped neckline and tiny sleeves, and Adanna looked adorably pretty in it.

Chapter 14

Later that evening Daniel poured two brandies and gave one to Alicia, poked up the fire, added a couple more logs and coal to the dancing flames, then dropped into the silky soft fabric of the sofa beside Alicia. He sighed contentedly. Alone together at last.

'How's your hand?' he asked, slipping his arm around her shoulders as if it was the most natural thing in the world. 'Still hurt?'

Alicia shook her head, feeling as if a bird was fluttering in her chest. Her hair bounced across her face and Daniel's long fingers swept it from her eyes, pushing it behind her ear. Smiling, he bent closer, pulled her gently into his embrace and kissed her fully on the lips, pushing his tongue into an open mouthed caress, feeding the passion between them. His heart was beating wildly and his head reeling from her taste, and the more he had, the hungrier he got for the rest of her. He brushed his warm lips over her eyes, around her ears, down her neck and across the silky skin of her breasts.

Alicia, her senses heating up as if she was on fire, half closed her eyes. Her skin seemed to sizzle where Daniel's lips had touched. Tendrils of hair were sticking to her neck; as he gently glided them aside and pressed his lips to her neck a fire shimmered in her core, provoking sensations she never knew existed as he discovered her erogenous zones. Suddenly she could hardly breathe; it felt too claustrophobic and she pushed against his chest. He immediately stopped and gazed into her eyes. He saw her nerviness and held her tenderly, soothing her like a small child.

'Why don't you tell me why I frighten you? Tell me what happened.'

She gazed up into his warm, loving eyes. 'I am not frightened of you, Daniel; I am frightened of myself.'

'Yourself?'

'And scared that if I tell you, you will not want me or be my friend.'

Daniel's eyebrows lifted and he looked long and hard into her blue lagoon eyes.

'Try me.'

She shook her head. 'I'm not sure I can.'

'You know about me and what I've done; now it is your turn. Come on; be brave.'

'It is not as simple as your ... I've killed people ... properly, deliberately, and I'm not sorry.'

Daniel blinked. That was the last thing he had expected Alicia to say. He swallowed hard. 'I expect it was self-defence. Something you had to do.'

Again Alicia shook her head, a cold calm entering her heart. 'I can see you are stunned ... I know you will hate me.' She moved out of his arms and made to stand up.

Daniel grasped her wrists and pulled her back onto the sofa. She did not even flinch at the tight hold he had on her injured hand, and when he looked into her face he saw the remote zombie eyes that he had often seen in the faces of the children in the camp compound. His heart twisted; this beautiful, caring person was half dead inside.

'I'm not here to judge you, Alicia. Just talk to me.'

Alicia's stiff body crumpled and she sat back into the folds of the settee. She looked into Daniel's eyes and knew that she would have to tell him … If she could. It could not rest between them now. She had never told anyone how she had murdered, how she had not only killed but mutilated those men in cold blood and with pleasure; well, not exactly pleasure but with satisfaction. Every killing had taken her further into her own dead being.

Daniel held her hands gently and waited patiently. His insides churned like milk turning to butter and the bile in his throat was the whey. He saw her make the decision in a split second. Fear clouded her eyes even as she smiled at him.

'I was just turned fifteen when my parents were murdered,' she began, her voice hardly audible as she stared into her lap. 'We had a holiday home in Yugoslavia, just over the border from Austria, in a small village. We had a lot of friends there, or so I thought. Mum inherited the house from her parents and we always went there for holidays.

'Dad was a doctor and had made friends with another doctor in the village, a Doctor Petrov Zerac. One night, without any warning, Zerac opened our front door and shot my parents straight through the head. Mum and Dad had been sitting curled up together on the settee watching TV and laughing. Mum had just called up to me in my bedroom to come down and kiss them goodnight as it was time for me to go to sleep. I had just started coming down the stairs and I saw them being shot. Petrov Zerac, with the gun still in his hand, stared up at me. I thought I was next, but he asked very calmly where my sister-in-law was. I answered just as calmly that she and my brother had gone away for the weekend and should be back tomorrow. There were my parents with their blood creeping all over the back of our cream settee and I was talking as if nothing out of the ordinary had happened!

'A young man was standing behind Zerac. Zerac turned to him and said he was to fetch me and put me in the truck with the others as I would be OK for the house down in Trieste. Then he instructed him to torch our house. The young man answered, "Yes, Uncle," and came towards the stairs. My feet were stuck to the stairs like glue. Zerac gave this sickly grin, then he shouted over his shoulder to his nephew as he turned and went out, giving him one last instruction, "Get a move on and bring her out the back entrance. We will come back tomorrow and get the foetus." My sister-in-law was five months pregnant.'

Alicia began rocking back and forth on the settee. 'I remember gazing down at Zerac's nephew. I had seen him at one of Zerac's famous garden parties that we had always gone to. His grin was even more sickly then his uncle's. He marched towards me and when I saw his eyes it somehow made me move. I twisted and raced up the stairs like it was some sort of game. I heard him laughing and telling me I couldn't get away and how he would enjoy me later.' Alicia looked up at Daniel for the first time and he saw the tangled emotions in her eyes as she recalled the memories. He wanted to hold her close and tell her to stop, but he knew she must spill as much as she could to stop the horror eating her up, so instead he rubbed her hand gently and said, 'Go on.'

Alicia now had a cine film of the events running through her head. She continued. 'Somehow I began to think rationally – Dad's influence; he always encouraged us to think clearly and calmly in a crisis or we would make things worse! Ha …' Alicia shook her head, her hair flying about her shoulders, as she questioned herself. 'Anyway, I tore up the stairs. The nearest door was my parents' room, not my bedroom, and I knew that Dad had a gun in his side drawer. There, how rational was that? I locked the bedroom door and raced to the drawer. My hands were trembling but somehow I managed to load the gun while Zerac's nephew was twisting the handle and banging on the door, laughing and calling me pretty names.

'Then he started yelling. He told me that he had started a fire downstairs and unless I opened the door we would both roast alive. When I still didn't open the door he kicked it open and sniggered when he saw me pointing the gun at him. He stepped towards me, saying I did not have the nerve to shoot him, and threw back his head, laughing. That was the last thing he said. I shot twice, I don't know why … I was the best marksperson in the family; better than Dad and my brother Brennen. Zerac's nephew just stared with his mouth open and an astonished look in his eyes and two bullet holes in his forehead, then slumped to the floor.

'I think it was the smell of the fire or something that made me move eventually, slowly at first, staring around the room as if my parents would appear and it would all turn out to be some awful nightmare. All I saw was a photo of Mum and Dad together looking happy. I pulled the photo off the wall, then grabbed more photos, some of me and Brennen and others of us all together. Then I ran like a mad person into my bedroom, found my rucksack and stuffed the photos inside along with all the pictures I could find from my room. Luckily I came across my passport and I rammed that into the bag too.

'By this time flames and thick black smoke were curling into my bedroom, mucking up my pink bedroom wallpaper that Dad had put up only a couple of weeks before. I remember staring at it. The paper turned brown like … as if … a cup of coffee had been thrown at it. Then I panicked, for the first time really, wondering how I was going to get downstairs against the flames, and I couldn't bear the thought of seeing my parents black and burnt. Suddenly I realised that I should climb out of the window, so I did.

'Looking around, I crept to the end of our garden. It was long, and we had bushes and trees and a big tree that was a sort of tree house with a small platform of branches. If I lay flat on the platform no one could see me. I knew this because I had often hidden from my parents there, especially at this time of year when the tree was in full leaf. The next thing I remember was Brennen waking me up. How could I have slept?'

It was then that Daniel gathered Alicia into his arms. She started in surprise, and Daniel stroked her hair slowly while she sobbed. It was his turn to wheedle out some of the darkness that she had hidden, just like she had done for him, he thought, although he wondered if it was possible to be free of such vast darkness. He doubted it, as did Adanna, but it was Shani, so mentally strong, who had said that you have to live with the blessings you now have. Daniel's eyes filled with unshed tears; his life and that of his wife's had been blessed. They had lived a life full of treasure with their son until that fateful night. They were lucky. He was lucky.

He lifted Alicia away from him and asked, 'Are you ready to go on?' He knew that if he asked if she wanted to go on she would say no, so he gave her no choice. She sat silently, wiping her tears with the tissue Daniel had given her. When she seemed unable to carry on, Daniel said, 'Tell me about Brennen. What was his wife's name?'

'Brennen was wonderful; fun and loving and always teasing me. He was seven years older than me. Mum lost a child, another brother, when he was only eighteen months old. He was born with something wrong with his heart. Then they had me. Brennen was the greatest brother, so full of happiness. I hated it when he went to uni to become a doctor like Dad. I missed him so much and so did Mum, so we extended our holiday for a few extra weeks so that we could spend more time together. The country had been mostly peaceful up until this point. Where we were living was quiet, but under the guise of conflict Zerac did his own sick business and killings.'

For a heartbeat Alicia was utterly still; she met Daniel's concerned eyes. Her lovely face twisted and her full beautiful lips curled. Her eyes, so blue before, were now dark and haunted. It was like exchanging stares with a statue. Daniel swallowed. Words vanished like wisps of smoke in autumn air. He felt as if his heart had been sucked out of his body, leaving only a hollow space. Alicia cast her eyes around the room like a trapped animal. She began again, her voice cracked with distress.

'Michelle was Brennen's wife's name. It should have been Angel, she was so sweet, with long blonde hair and grey eyes. She was a couple of years older than Brennen, a primary school teacher; she was magic with children.' Tears started tumbling over Alicia's cheeks again.

'She would have made a great mum. Instead Zerac and his men raped her, butchered her and cut the baby out of her stomach. I heard her screams in the woods and most nights in my head. Brennen had decided to drive us all to the airport. We should have gone the other way to the Austrian border after my parents' murder and got out of the country back to England as fast as we could. Apart from our burnt house the village looked untouched when we escaped.

'Brennen and Michelle had come for a couple of month's holiday before she started a new job. Some holiday; they never got back to England. Zerac and his 'business' partners had followed us, but we didn't know that. We stopped for the night in some empty old lodge in the woods because Michelle was hot, being sick and not feeling well, probably from fear and shock. Brennen asked me to go and collect some kindling to light a fire while he made up a bed for Michelle. He gave me Dad's gun and told me to be careful and not go too far away, although we didn't know we were in any danger. We thought that we had got away from the fighting. It was not until much later that I found out that there had been no fighting – at least, not in our village and not involving civilians. It was Zerac taking his opportunity for his repugnant pursuit.

'I had just found enough kindling when I heard Michelle screaming. I went to run back, but her screams became a cry that was so unearthly and horrendous that I stopped. After the screams I heard several gunshots, then everything seemed quiet in the lodge by the time I crept back.'

Alicia, her voice high-pitched, burst forth: 'I was such a coward! I stayed hidden in the woods, watching and scared, cradling the kindling. I saw several men building a fire outside the lodge; then Zerac and more men came out. There were nine men in all, including Zerac and his son. I nearly approached them then, thinking that Brennen and Michelle were OK. I half dismissed the screaming as Michelle just being frightened. The men were all laughing and if I hadn't actually seen Zerac shoot my parents I might have gone up to them.

'Suddenly, though, they made a spit over the fire and fetched what I realised was Michelle's dead baby and started smoking it over the flames. I knew then that Michelle was dead. I thought they were going to eat the foetus and I couldn't stop vomiting as I watched and shivered. Then I just shut down. I didn't feel the cold, my hunger, nothing, but I noted all their faces. Faces I shall never forget. They stay with me in my dreams. I see them roasting Brennen's child in the evening sunlight and into the flickering firelight of the night … Along with the smell of burning flesh. I never slept. I just watched them all that night until they moved off in the early hours of the morning. After they had gone and taken the smoked baby I managed somehow to make myself go into the lodge with some hope that Brennen and even Michelle were OK.

'Michelle was tied to the bed in a sea of blood with her belly sliced open. Her face was as white as bone, her eyes were sunken and a small trickle of dried blood was stuck to the corner of her mouth. She was dead. Brennen had been shot twice and had a large cut down his face. He had obviously tried to fight back; he was tied to a chair and had also bled profusely. He was barely alive.

'I untied him, held him in my arms and his eyes flicked open. His voice was hardly audible but it seemed to shatter the silence in the lodge like breaking glass. "It was Zerac again. Go as fast as you can to the airport, back to England, to Granddad. Zerac thinks you are dead." Then his eyes travelled towards Michelle and his face crumpled up with pain. "Look what they did to my beautiful Michi." Then he gasped and his head fell back further into my arms. For a moment he looked as if he was asleep but I knew he had died.

'When I was able I dragged him onto the bed next to Michelle, curled their stiff bodies together and set fire to them. At least they were with Mum and Dad then.'

At last Alicia glanced up at Daniel. He looked back at her with the expressionless stare of an overgrown child.

'I've never, ever told anyone what happened next. Maybe I shouldn't?'

Daniel shook his head, words locked in his throat, and somehow gave her a weak smile. He rubbed the back of her hand with his long fingers.

Reassured, Alicia took a deep breath before continuing. 'It was as if a madness suddenly came over me. Within two days my family had been wiped out, murdered like a film on TV or a video game. But this was no game. War is not a game to those who live in it. I wanted revenge. I cared nothing for my life. I felt dead anyhow and I wanted those vile men dead. I caught up with them the next day, driving Dad's car that Brennen had driven into the woods. They were heading towards the Slovenia–Croatia border.

'I caught up first with Edin, Petrov Zerac's son. We knew each other well. He was only nineteen and he often flirted with me at parties and if he saw me in the village. He was alone when I found him, which was just as well really as I had no plan, just this burning flame of hate. No, it was more than that, and it was deep inside my belly; in my heart, in my very soul, if I still had one, and I didn't care for my own life, which made me even deadlier. Edin was calmly sitting in an old wicker chair outside a derelict house. Lots of houses had been left by people fleeing from the area. He was drinking coffee when he spotted me coming towards him and he nearly choked on it. "Thought you were dead," were his first words. "Dad will be surprised." He was grinning widely and I saw the lust in his eyes as I closed in on him.

'"I was looking for my brother. Have you seen him?"

'He shook his head but couldn't meet my eyes.

'"Want some coffee?"

'I nodded and he turned and went into the kitchen. I followed, and while he was pouring the hot coffee into the cup and had his back turned I came up behind him, put Dad's gun against his head and fired. Warm blood and bone sprayed over my face and up the walls and mingled with the liquid from the broken cup of coffee when he collapsed to the floor. I remember wondering what colour the dark coffee and the dark blood would make together. Then rage hit me. I grabbed a kitchen knife, tore off his trousers and cut off his manhood like I was filleting a fish or a rabbit, just like Dad and Brennen had taught me when we had gone hunting. I stuck it in his mouth.

'I even went to the sink and washed the knife clean afterwards. Then I caught a glimpse of myself covered in blood in the reflection of the window like it was someone else's shadow. Looking down at Edin, I realised that I had changed that day into someone else who I no longer recognised. Then I started looking casually around the rooms as if I was some sort of estate agent instead of a cold-blooded murderer.

'I suddenly noticed a large wooden crate – a box of grenades. I took half a dozen. Next to the crate was another box. I grabbed several guns and bullets and stuffed them all into my rucksack. On the wall in the sitting room above the fireplace was a sword. I took it down and slashed it through the air, then across one of the armchairs. The blade was deadly sharp and the material sprung, curling, from the slash I had made in the cushion. Then I went back for the kitchen knife.

'I hid Dad's car further into the woods, although it was nearly out of petrol and would not get me much further, then came back and hid in the vacant house opposite. Petrov Zerac drove up in his gleaming four-by-four with a couple of other men. I recognised one of them from the night before. Zerac breezed into the house calling his son's name, then came out vomiting and collapsed onto the chair that Edin had been sitting in. He looked mighty upset.' Alicia smiled at the picture in her head of Petrov Zerac's horror struck face. Now in robot mode, her eyes as bright as a blazing star and fixed at a point beyond Daniel, she blurted it all out.

'I tracked them *all* down and executed them all, and finished them off like I had Edin. Except for Petrov Zerac. I still haven't found him … Yet.'

Daniel gasped. Alicia shifted, becoming aware of Daniel and his sitting room. Returning to reality, she stole a glance at Daniel. He looked pale and tears were streaming down his face.

Well, that's that with Daniel, she thought to herself. Her heart felt as heavy and cold as stone. She unlaced her fingers from Daniel's and got up from the sofa like an old woman. She drew a great breath and let it out slowly. I've told someone I am a murderer. Now it is up to him if he wants to tell the authorities.

She gave a quick laugh without mirth and flung her eyes to the ceiling, daring those above her to … what? She suddenly didn't care. She felt drained and enormously weary.

Not looking at Daniel, she headed for the front door and found her jacket hanging on the hall stand. As she slipped it on, Daniel was suddenly beside her.

'Are you going home?' he asked in a cracked voice.

'I think it's best. I expect I'm not the sort of woman you want around your children.'

Daniel didn't reply. Alicia sighed and opened the front door.

Laying a hand on her slight shoulder he said, 'It is such a shock. I can't quite take it in.' He gazed into her eyes and saw the compassion for him in the swirls of deep blue.

'But it was a long time ago in a different world. Who knows what anyone would have done. Stay.'

'Are you sure?' Alicia asked, her eyes wide in surprise.

Daniel nodded. In his mind he could not imagine Alicia deliberately killing anyone; she was so caring. The woman he knew, or felt he knew, was no assassin who cut people up. She couldn't even cut up meat!

Walking back into the sitting room he downed his brandy and poured himself a second. Glancing over his shoulder, he gestured to Alicia. Did she want another? She shook her head, sitting stiffly on the edge of the sofa, still wearing her blue jacket that matched her eyes. She watched his every move. Memories of the compound children came flooding into Daniel's brain again. However, as much as he tried, he couldn't, just couldn't see Alicia murdering anyone, let alone mutilating a dead body.

Suddenly she spoke. 'Are you going to tell the police?'

'Good lord, no. I can see you had justification ... I just can't believe ... it's hard to imagine ...'

'That I'm not the sweet innocent person you thought I was?'

'Something like that. Did you find out why they wanted a foetus? Why did they smoke it and take it with them?'

Alicia chewed on her bottom lip for a moment before answering. 'The whole Zerac family were collecting foetuses and smoking them. Then they would gold leaf them and sell them to Thai families for hundreds of pounds. They are a good luck symbol there. They had a house full of woman that they raped and made pregnant. Then, when they were about five months, they would slit their stomachs and take out the live foetus. They did this several times until the women either died or they sold them as sex slaves. I blew all the Zerac family and their 'business' premises to hell where they all belonged.'

Daniel's knees suddenly felt weak and he slumped onto the settee beside Alicia. Some human beings were a species all to themselves, beyond evil! He thought chopping off hands and butchering people was bad enough; now this.

'What makes people do that? What kind of doctor … What kind of man …?'

'That's not all they did. They would let some of the women go on and have the babies, then sell them, and if any baby died, and apparently a lot did, they would grind up their bones and sell that for medicine.'

Oh God! No wonder, he thought, that Alicia did what she did. She was the bravest woman he had ever met. Then he thought of Shani. She was brave too. Women were brave; in some countries they were treated like non-beings, but they were the better half of the human race.

Daniel looked at Alicia's pale face. She was starved of love; she had no family left to love her. Even her granddad had died only a couple of years after she had returned to England. She had scars in her heart as bad as Adanna's; no wonder they got on so well. They had both seen their parents murdered in front of them and then …

Adanna might have reacted in the same way if she had not been captured and surrounded by soldiers. Although as he looked at Alicia, now in a completely different way, he knew that she had more passion, was not as accepting and submissive as Adanna. In Adanna's culture women were more submissive compared with Alicia's western world. Alicia would have fought them all and died in the process rather than submit. Then he remembered his murderous rage towards the man who had let Shani die by not allowing her on the plane. He would have killed him if no one had pulled him away. How could he condemn Alicia when he could easily have done the same? Love, to Daniel, cured everyone, and that was what he would do. He loved the children and they were slowly healing. So would Alicia if he loved her.

'What are you thinking?' Alicia said in a tiny voice, tears glistening in the corners of her blue eyes; blue like the sea, crystal clear blue – now shimmering, crashing and churning.

'How beautiful your eyes are.'

Alicia blushed, but didn't move. The first move would have to come from Daniel. She had completely shut down. In the whirligig of her mind only horror had the upper hand.

Daniel bent his lean body towards her and kissed her gently on her soft cheek. When she smiled at him he pulled her into his arms and held her against his pounding chest. She settled there like a kitten finding a comfortable warm corner. That was how they found themselves in the early hours of the morning. Cuddled together on the settee with the embers of the dying fire in the grate.

As Alicia moved away from Daniel's warm body she shivered, but she had slept soundly all night; not one dream. Nothing but blankness like pale shadows. It was as if pouring out her sins had washed her of them, at least for a while.

Daniel moaned, still half asleep, when she moved. 'Where are you going?'

'To the loo.'

'Oh, mmm. It has got cold in here,' he said, scrambling up, his hair wild and tousled. 'I will make you a hot water bottle and you can take it up to the spare room. The children will be awake soon.'

'But it is not five o'clock yet.'

Daniel gave a deep chuckle. 'Mmm, but Jobi will be up at six. You will be lucky to get any more sleep. My advice to you is to keep your head underneath the covers, which may work, although he was so excited at you staying the night, I bet you will be his first port of call.'

'I won't mind. I'm surprised I slept so well. Usually I don't and especially after …'

'Don't let's talk about last night,' Daniel cut in, 'unless you really need to talk it out more. I think we should move on.'

'What, together, or just friends … What?'

'Let's try together.'

Alicia eyebrows rose, wrinkling her forehead. 'You sure?'

'Don't you want to?'

'Oh, yes,' tears threatened to spill.

'Shoo, to the loo then. I'll get you a bottle.'

Obediently Alicia padded across the carpet in her bare feet and nearly skipped out of the room, her heart unfrozen and filling up with love. No wonder she loved Daniel. He was so understanding, so tender and so decent and warm. Absolutely magnificent!

However, Daniel was thinking that the sooner what Alicia had told him slipped from his mind the better. He told himself that she had been ill, mentally ill – who wouldn't have been? – and she did not know what she was doing, killing all those men. It was a question of survival - instinct. He dismissed the thought that she had gone after the men, which was not exactly survival. As he poured the boiling water into the rubber bottle, he reassured himself that all she needed was love. She was not the same person … child … that had … Anyhow, he was unable to resist her whatever she had done in the past, *and* it was in the past.

'Are you sure I need this bottle? It is summer, you know,' giggled Alicia. Daniel nodded, and when she slipped out of her dress and shyly and very quickly jumped in between the cotton sheets, Daniel tucked her in like a child, just as her parents had done. Love for this man washed over her.

'I think I am in love with you,' she said as he bent and kissed her softly on her lips.

Daniel grinned, 'That's good because I think I'm in love with you too. Now go back to sleep. I'll see you in the morning – well, later.'

Sleep would not come to Daniel. He stared up at the ceiling as he lay with his hands under his head contemplating the things that Alicia had said about the Zerac family. How could anyone be that black-hearted and feed on such demonic acts just for money? Looking back at his childhood, and even his life until he had gone to Africa, he perceived how he had been sheltered from unholy evil. And popping into his brain came the saying that his grandmother used to quote: 'Money is the root of all evil'.

Then there was Alicia; how could he begin to identify her with the girl she had told him about? A girl who killed not just once! A girl so broken and dead that it was beyond his understanding. Was she still that person, a person he should keep away from his children? Suddenly his thoughts were interrupted by the squeak of a bedroom door followed by soft, padding footsteps. He heard Jobi say to Alicia, 'Are you awake under there?' and he heard Alicia say, 'Boo.' Jobi erupted into giggles and must have jumped into bed with Alicia, as she shrieked that his feet were like ice. Daniel smiled to himself. Yes, all she needed was love.

Chapter 15

It was late Friday afternoon before she heard from Daniel again. He phoned and said he would pick her up about seven-thirty.

'Do you know where I live?'

'Well, roughly; and I have your address. See you later.'

Alicia had wondered whether Daniel would cancel their date and she had been half-expecting a phone call with excuses. They had all gone their separate ways on the Wednesday morning after having breakfast, and as Daniel piled the children, bags and books into the car he had said, as an afterthought Alicia thought, 'See you Friday night then.'

On that Wednesday morning at work she had found it too hard to help her clients and in the end she had to cancel her afternoon appointments, giving the excuse of not feeling well, which was not far from the truth. Then that night she had hardly slept at all, the flashbacks searing through her mind like an electric knife. Even when she woke they would not stop, and last night had not been any easier. Talking to Daniel had opened the deep wounds that skulked about in her head.

She looked hollow-eyed and she knew it. Now, as she stared into the mirror, she noticed dark rings around her eyes as if someone had punched her. She took several hours choosing what to wear. This was her first date ever, and so much had changed between her and Daniel. Eventually she settled for grey velvet trousers and a blue, cream and grey top with a slightly scooped neckline. She wore her hair piled up and put blue sparkly earrings in her ears. She chose grey high-heeled shoes that made her long legs look even longer. When it came to make-up, she highlighted her eyes with pale blue, hoping that the colour would detract from the dark puffy rings. When she stared into the mirror again she convinced herself that it had worked.

When Daniel turned up he was wearing cream trousers and a brown shirt that emphasised his warm brown eyes. He grinned with pleasure like a schoolboy when she opened the door, and handed her a huge bunch of wild flowers.

'The children's idea, from the garden,' he said almost apologetically.

'They're beautiful and smell wonderful. I'll put them in a vase. Would you like a drink before we go?'

'No thanks, the table is booked for eight,' he answered.

Alicia, already nervous, felt like screaming. Daniel was being very formal; no kiss, not even on the cheek when he gave her the flowers. Then she realised that she was being just as unfriendly. For a moment she thought about cancelling their date, but one glance at how handsome Daniel looked and she changed her mind. After arranging the flowers in a vase, she placed them on the glass coffee table. Daniel smiled his approval and she picked up her blue jacket and bag.

'Right. I'm ready.'

'Got your keys?'

Alicia nodded.

'Your house looks nice. I see it is up for sale.'

'Yes. I'm hoping to move closer to the beach. I put it on the market a month ago and I've only had one person come and look.'

'Yes, it is not the best of times to sell. The market is very slow.'

'Yes, apparently it could be as long as a year before I sell it. I loved it here for so long but I have new next-door neighbours with four teenagers. They have spoilt my peace and quiet. They play music at all hours and come in late and drunk, shouting, swearing and banging doors. And their back garden is overgrown and rubbish and old chairs are piling up. I have put up a taller fence and I spoke to the parents but they were abusive. Life is too short to put up with neighbours like that.'

'I'm sorry. Maybe you will be lucky and move quickly.'

'Only if people visit on a day when they are all out.'

'Well, neighbours from hell is not a selling point, granted.'

'Hell is not my neighbours,' Alicia muttered quietly.

Daniel pretended not to hear. The last thing he wanted to do was to bring up anything about her past. He was still trying to process it. At night he had been having haunted dreams of the fear that he had felt when they fled Africa, Shani's butchered body all mixed up in his mind with Alicia and some shadowy male figures.

Daniel held the car door open for Alicia to climb in. He noticed that she looked very tired. Somehow he hoped to bring her sparkle back. Then he thought that maybe her previous sparkle had been a pretence. He wanted to sigh but managed to hold it in, and then he gazed at her lovely face and his trousers tightened like they always did when she was near.

The dinner was scrumptious and the restaurant was decorated glamorously in shades of cream and brown with red cushions, vases and pictures. After a couple of glasses of wine they both loosened up and began teasing each other and giggling together. By the time they left they were like a different couple and, when Alicia invited him in for coffee, Daniel accepted her invitation.

She put some soft music on and poured the coffee. As she straightened up, Daniel grabbed her and pulled her onto his lap. She giggled and they started giving each other gentle little kisses. When she felt how hard he was against her, proof of how much he wanted her, she nearly asked him upstairs, but felt too shy to do so. She also wondered if she would get another attack of the claustrophobic panic she had felt on Tuesday night.

Daniel was very aware of how he had to go slow this time and keep his feelings in check, although that was harder than he envisaged. He wanted to take Alicia and explore her warm, sexy body and delve inside her. He gave her light kisses and teasingly bit her lower lip. When she squirmed, he gently nibbled her right ear.

'Oh I could eat you, you are so delicious,' he said, stopping his kisses, mostly to control himself and his hammering heart. He leaned forward, shifting Alicia to the right of his bulge and, with slightly shaking hands, picked up his coffee mug, unsuccessfully trying to seem casual.

Alicia was not sure how to respond for a moment but she badly wanted to carry on touching and kissing. She saw how shaky Daniel was and suddenly courage soared through her. She started kissing the side of his neck and felt him quiver, which gave her more confidence. She also found his self-restraint seductive. She gave a soft *meow* and rubbed her face against his cheek like a cat. She chuckled when she heard him groan.

'Your coffee is getting cold,' Daniel stated, holding onto his mug tightly.

'So is yours because you are not drinking it. Anyhow I don't really want mine.'

Daniel looked deeply at Alicia and she gave him a wicked grin, which resulted in him nearly missing the glass-topped table as he put his full mug down on it. When their lips touched she melted into him, slipping her hands into his shirt, and things instantly went wild. Their tongues collided feverishly and their kissing was hard, wet and desperate. Daniel started stroking her back and cradling her bottom. Alicia's nerve endings crackled and made it hard for her to breathe. Their gazes met and Daniel saw unguarded desire cross her face.

'Either I had better go or we should go upstairs to bed,' he said, pulling his lips away from hers.

'Go upstairs,' Alicia murmured into his ear as she continued kissing his mouth. 'Or are you expected home?'

Daniel scooped her further into his arms. 'No. Mrs Jones is staying the night, but I didn't say because I didn't want to assume …' and he gently gathered her enticing body to his and carried her upstairs.

'Bedroom?' he enquired between her warm lips and his.

Alicia pointed. When they were beside her bed he slid her feet gently to the ground. 'Can I?' he asked, as his fingers went to the zip at the back of her blouse. Alicia nodded up at him. He pulled her against his hard chest and slid the zip down the back of her blouse, then dragged a finger slowly down her spine. She gave a sensuous shiver and her nipples went hard. Panic never entered her mind this time; sexual lust zinged through her body when she smelt the tang of Daniel's aftershave, and his male scent overrode any feelings of claustrophobia.

Together they fell back onto the soft silk of her bedspread and Daniel drifted kisses over her eyes and down the soft white skin of her throat. He undid her bra and a perky breast fell out; he cupped it with the palm of his hand. After removing her bra, he lifted her soft mound and took her hard nipple into the hot cavern of his mouth while fondling her other breast. Tingles shot up her legs and settled in her insides for a brief moment.

Daniel kissed her belly as he glided her pants off, sending goose bumps all over her from head to toe. Then he traced a path with his lips from her inner thigh to the junction of her legs, coasting down to her intimate part between her legs, which he gently parted so that he could skim down her long legs to her toes. She lay motionless with her eyes closed, drinking in the sensations that he was evoking across her body as his lips and slim fingers explored every crevice. All thoughts of any past or present were blasted away by the out-of-control fire in her brain.

When Daniel had finished tasting her, a self-satisfied smile on his face and his eyes smouldering, he took both of her perky nipples between his fingers and rubbed them tenderly until she became so aroused that she felt herself moistening. When he gazed into her eyes, passion ignited.

Alicia's body, fully awake, went utterly still as Daniel tried pushing himself into her. When she cried out in distress as Daniel broke her virginal wall it was several seconds before he became aware of what had happened.

'You're a virgin!'

'What, still?'

'No ...'

Their bodies laced together, they moved into the depths of desire as their hips jerked, affection and love unfolding like a flower in Alicia's heart. She felt as dizzy as a cloud, the past and reality floating off into a bottomless void in her mind, casting off the cloak of cold darkness. Loneliness faded away.

Daniel pulled the bedspread over their perspiring bodies and they both collapsed into the cotton sheets, clinging together like ivy. His face lit up and chuckles of joy bubbled out of him as he gathered Alicia into his arms. He had completely lost the plot and gone up like a rocket, discharging emotions he never knew had existed in him, when he discovered that Alicia was a virgin and all his. He kissed her full lips with such tenderness that her body began to heat up and melt all over again. As her lips clung to his, she wondered how it was possible to be so easily lost in the music of love.

Daniel, between kisses which he seemed to be unable to stop, whispered, 'Oh, you are so wonderful and all mine. I can't believe it … All mine; every bit of you.'

'I will always be yours,' Alicia murmured against his hot kisses. 'I'm going to try and stop feeding on old bad memories and make some new good ones so that other good memories might return.' And in that instant it seemed so simple.

'And I promise to try and take you there,' he said, love beaming out of every pore. She gave him a surprised look, like a child catching an older person in a foolish statement. A hundred reasons why that couldn't happen played fitfully in her head like fingers running over a keyboard.

Daniel arched a brow. 'You are feeding on the bad memories.' And he gave her a lingering open-mouthed kiss to fill the need inside her. Her heart thundered and her senses reeled. when she came up for air her mood had changed, and when she looked at Daniel it seemed as if the air was filled with his smiles.

Alicia slept for most of the night wrapped up in Daniel's arms. Occasionally she would whimper, and Daniel stroked her hair and gave her tiny kisses until she drifted back to sleep. When he woke her in the morning with kisses down the side of her neck, her eyes popped open and she turned startled before she glimpsed Daniel grinning above her.

'Sorry,' she said, and settled back into his arms. 'I'm not used to waking with a man in my bed.'

'My God,' gasped Daniel, his eyes travelling to the bed clothes, and Alicia saw that the sheets and their naked bodies were plastered in shades of red blood. 'It looks like a massacre.'

'Oh, is this normal?' asked Alicia.

'Well, mmm, yes; you are nearly twenty-eight, I suppose.'

'How about your wife or other women; have they been like this?' Alicia said, embarrassed.

'I've never met a virgin before.'

'What about your wife?'

'No, Catherine had had several relationships before she met me.'

'Oh.'

'Oh indeed,' Daniel said, noticing Alicia's eyes beginning to glisten. 'A bit old-fashioned, a bit caveman-like I suppose, but I'm thrilled that you were a virgin and are all mine.'

'You are?'

'Of course. Now you stay there while I run you a bath. I'll have a shower and you can tell me where the clean bed sheets are and I'll sort out the bed. Let's hope there is not too much of a stain on the mattress.'

Daniel insisted that Alicia come home with him for the weekend. He treated her like a delicate china doll until he gave her breakfast in bed on Sunday morning, when she burst out laughing at his concern.

'Enough, Daniel,' she giggled as he sliced the top off her boiled egg, the children tucked into bed on either side of her. 'I'm fine now – honest. The children want to go down to the beach and it is such a beautiful warm day, I think we should go.'

'Only if you are feeling well enough,' Adanna said, looking up anxiously at her father.

'Where is our breakfast?' Jobi asked. 'I feel unwell too. I think I have caught Alicia's virus.'

'Oh, you do, do you? Well, your breakfast is downstairs on the table. If you think you have a virus, you had better not come with us to the beach.'

Jobi's big eyes sparkled. He was well able to beat his dad at this game. 'When I have my breakfast it will give me energy to get up and make the virus go.'

'Mmm, I see. Looks like breakfast in bed all round then,' grinned Daniel, revelling in the picture of all the people he loved looking so cosy together.

The sun shone scorching hot, like a great gold dragon writhing in the shimmering blue sky. The sparkling sea was warm and inviting enough for them all to go swimming, even Squirt, who, after coaxing from Adanna, came paddling furiously towards her, his head as high as he could manage, before jumping into her arms. They laughed and played around in the surf with Alicia while Daniel dragged Jobi out on his body board before letting him go, giggling hysterically as he skimmed the long and lazy rolling waves to the white foam that swept the shore, only to plead with his father to take him back out so he could do it again.

Later Alicia took Adanna and Jobi to investigate the rock- pools with Squirt, who gazed into the pools wondering why everyone was peering into the glassy water. When he saw his reflection he began to bark and dance about and promptly slipped into the pool, much to Jobi's annoyance because Squirt 'scared' all the creatures living in the pool. Not as though they had found any creatures to scare!

Adanna soon got fed up and went back to join Daniel, who was snoozing under a sun umbrella. Of course, Squirt followed her and, finding Daniel lying flat out on the sand, immediately gave him loving licks all over his face. Not only was his face horribly wet but golden sand had showered like hail from Squirt's damp, velvety body and waving tail, covering Daniel's features. He grabbed the wriggling puppy, scolding him, but it did no good; the pup had missed him for a whole fifteen minutes!

Chapter 16

During the following days Alicia felt so happy and loved that the horrific dreams about her family and the men she had killed retreated. She dreamt only of Daniel.

She and Daniel could not keep their hands off each other. Their lovemaking, after the first couple of nights when he had been gentle and patient, became wild. Alicia's passion for him danced like fire. Love was like having a virus, she thought one day as she rushed to see him. It flies and grows white-hot and throws your body into turmoil, sensations going haywire. Even if he just smiled at her, her legs felt weak.

They spent every bit of their spare time together. Even when they were at work they couldn't stop thinking about each other. Daniel, who had first loved his wife Catherine and then Shani, could not understand his passion for Alicia. It was like a vessel that he could not fill up.

Also Daniel absolutely hated it when he could not get a sitter and she had to stay at her own house. Poor Mrs Jones was unavailable for so many nights and his parents were on a world cruise. After three weeks of Alicia sleeping in the spare bed whenever she stopped at his house, which was *every* weekend, she finally moved into his bed as he could not bear her being next door. So Alicia gradually moved in with Daniel and the children … oh, and Squirt, he being as devoted to Alicia as Daniel.

Having moved in together, Daniel thought his feelings for Alicia might calm down a bit, but they didn't. In insane moments he wondered if it was because he had had both his previous loves for such a short time and unconsciously feared that the same would happen with Alicia. At other times, when he was away from her just thinking about her made his trousers tighten. The laughter between them, which seemed almost constant, was like sunshine inside his heart. He thought their lovemaking was extraordinary. It had been good with Catherine and Shani but, with Alicia it was like being on another plane. He was always completely out of control.

They settled down together as a family and seemed quite normal to all outside appearances. Alicia and Daniel spent their free days making love in bed while the children were at school, or strolling along the beach with Squirt, hand in hand. They went out for romantic evenings together when Mrs Jones was able to babysit, and they intermingled their friends as a couple.

Daniel had never felt so close to another living soul before. There was an affinity between them like she was half of him. In the beginning he thought it was because she had been a virgin and had never belonged to anyone else, but it was more than that. They laughed so much together, yet they could be together in silence, speech unnecessary between them. He also loved the moments when Alicia slumbered in his arms in bed while he watched. When she moved from his arms it felt like an empty cradle. She threw her love for him and for the children about her like warm rain in the tropics.

Family life consisted of Adanna and Alicia doing self-defence classes together while Daniel took Jobi swimming.

They went to the cinema together once a fortnight to watch a funny film, as anything that had violence or war upset Adanna, with a 'non-healthy' meal, as Daniel called it, to follow. He ate as much chips and burger as they did, though! They all went cycling, Jobi, Alicia and Daniel did gardening together, and Alicia and Adanna cooked together, although Alicia had to admit that Adanna was the best of cooks and far better than her. Adanna now took Jobi regularly to the village shop, and always came back with the local gossip, as Mrs Kapur never let even a fly get past her! Adanna often went, by herself, across the field behind Daniel's house to the edge of the woods walking Squirt, who was growing fast.

Alicia moving in with the family had a positive effect on Adanna too, and during the following months she started slowly changing. She managed to go for whole days, and even the occasional night, without fearing the commander. And at last she began thinking like other teenagers; her mind was filled with wanting to look nice, which amazed her, as after she had been sexually abused she hadn't wanted to look attractive or pretty at all in case some male found her desirable. However, with Alicia's daily counselling she began to feel good about herself when she knew she looked lovely. As Alicia explained, looking attractive had nothing to do with the violence of rape and abuse; that was about power and control.

So Adanna started trying different hair designs, and she loved having her nails painted. She joined her school friends' world by inviting some of them home for girly evenings and sleepovers at Alicia's suggestion, and although she refused to stay the night at any of her friends' houses she would visit them and join them for teen days. She also enjoyed going shopping with Alicia – that is, for clothes;

when it came to food shopping she was not so keen! She and Jobi made excuses for not going, like homework that they didn't really have. However, the ruse worked well with Daniel and Alicia. She was put 'in charge' of Jobi, and as soon as the grownups disappeared they would slump on the settee and eat as much rubbish as they could find while watching TV and playing video games. Yes, Adanna was becoming a normal teenager. Her confidence around people was increasing too. She was no longer afraid of this new world and the people she met.

As a family they would often get 'looks' because of the children's dark skin next to a white mother and mixed-race father, but Adanna never experienced blatant prejudice until she went ten pin bowling to celebrate the birthday of her friend, an Indian girl. She went with her friend's parents and several of her other new school friends. As they were playing, a group of boys who were bowling on the next lane started calling Adanna and her friend names because they were dark-skinned.

When Adanna looked distressed, her friend's father sat her down and said, with his arm around her shoulder, 'There will always be times when ignorant people like them will only see the colour of your skin and will be nasty. The best way to handle it is to ignore them and pity them for their ignorance. Being black will always cause comments; we have put up with it all our lives.'

Adanna was surprised that she did not feel the urge to run home and find Daniel. She did feel nervous when the boys glanced at her – until her friend poked her tongue out at them and was scolded by her father, who said in a very loud voice, so that the boys could hear, 'There is no need to stoop to their level of rudeness and vulgarity.' After that the boys packed up being insulting towards them and eventually finished their game and shuffled away.

That night Adanna thought the episode might cause her to have a bad dream. She thought that the nastiness might cause her to dream about the day she watched her birth parents slashed and killed. But instead she dreamt about her parents and her brothers on a good day, when they had all gone into the fields and picked vegetables for their dinner and ended up chasing each other, creasing up with laughter until their tummies hurt.

Not for the first time she wondered what had happened to her brothers. She felt guilty about leaving them behind, and sometimes had visions of them being chopped up, their blood spurting in all directions until it flowed towards her trying to drown her. At other times she saw them teasing her, and even felt her little brother clinging to her as she held him on her hip. She made up her mind that she needed to find out about her brothers.

The following day she told Alicia what had happened at the bowling alley and said that it had led her to have a good dream and that she wondered if she could somehow find out whether her brothers were alive or dead. Before, she had been too frightened to make contact with anyone in her homeland in case the commander found out she was still alive. Now she knew that even if he did, he would not come to England for her, and even if he came he would not be able to take her and abuse her again. She would die first. Yes, the fear of him had gone, even though seeing him slice up her parents and what he had done to her would never leave her.

For the first time since she had rolled into the hospital compound, her stomach filled with a child, her insides stopped churning. Her fear evaporated that day in the early morning light. That morning she even grieved a little for the baby until she thought it might be like the commander; then hate raged in her heart. She felt anger for the first time, letting it pour over her like a trembling flood.

Alicia was full of praise for Adanna for not feeling afraid and for not going backwards in her progress because of the bowling episode. That made Adanna feel good too, and she confided in Alicia about her anger. Together they explored her feelings until Adanna realised that the anger was a stepping stone towards a new her – a person who could have many different emotions again. It was a normal reaction even if it had been delayed.

Then Alicia promised to try and trace her brothers if she could. Later that night, in bed, she discussed it with Daniel.

'I think it would help Adanna to know what has happened to her brothers. She feels guilty about her survival and about living here so well. Also, maybe it would be kind if you found out what has happened to Jobi's uncles, Shani's two boys. You told me you promised to help find them. Just because she is dead you should not forget your promise to her.'

'Yes, you are right. We should help Adanna to find out about her brothers, but Jobi hardly remembers Shani let alone his uncles.' Then, in a cracked voice, he added, 'But again, my promise to Shani should be kept. She deserves that from me.'

Alicia slipped her hand over his bare shoulder and he turned towards her, her jet hair spread out across the pillow, small ringlets framing her oval features. Daniel reached out and fondled one of the sprigs as they chatted.

'You have looked after Shani's grandson and loved him like your own; she would thank you for that,' said Alicia.

'Mmm, but I promised her more than that. I shall look for her sons,' Daniel said. He didn't want to think about Shani. Like thoughts of his wife and son, it brought frosty shadows and turned his stomach icy. He wrapped his strong arms around Alicia and drew her warm body close to his chest, feeling her naked breasts soft against his skin. Her breasts had always enchanted him. They were small, but round and plump, not heavy but perky, a little like prepubescent breasts, with large strawberry nipples. He met her gaze as she looked up at him; his penis jumped to life and she grinned.

'I will get in touch with some contacts tomorrow,' Daniel promised.

'Mmm, and me too,' Alicia said as Daniel covered her lips with his. His tongue prised open her mouth and searched for hers. A frisson of tingles zinged through her and her ripe nipples went shamelessly rigid. She immediately started to moisten and her heartbeat went into overdrive. Daniel shifted his attention to her neck, then gave her a series of scorching kisses along her arms.

He turned her onto her stomach and kissed each vertebra of her backbone until she gave a little moan. Then, twisting her onto her back, he made his way to her right soft mound. She pushed her nipple deep into his mouth as he sucked desperately, at the same time cupping her left breast and rubbing her nipple with his slim finger.

She started to squirm in a delirium of arousal, reaching down to find his hard rod. He repositioned himself and slid inside her. Their thighs bumped together and their hips jerked, carnal desire driving them on until they both burst and fell away from each other, breathing rapidly.

Calming down, Daniel turned to Alicia, coasted his arm under her neck, tucked her long hair behind her ear and sought her face. She threw him a smile, her eyes still dancing. He returned his boyish lopsided grin.

'I have no idea why it is that I cannot control myself with you. I'm a slave to your body. I've never found anyone so alluring. It's been like this since I first saw you. That first day I wanted you so much that I had a hard job concentrating on what you were saying.'

'I felt the same, but I was amazed when you asked me out. I'm even more staggered that you can love me when I have had such a past.'

'I can't associate you with such actions,' Daniel said, as his insides did a somersault. 'You are too caring, with the most wonderful way of throwing your love at all of us.'

'Do you want your own children, Daniel?'

'You mean father my own again, with you?'

'Yes. I would like your child, but later down the line a bit, if we last.'

'Why shouldn't we last? And yes, I think I would like children with you. Shall we start practising now?' A mischievous sparkle came into his eyes.

'Oh, and here's me thinking you have had enough of me for tonight,' Alicia teased, and rolled towards Daniel. He embraced her in his athletic arms and slid a finger down her spine. She shivered and goose pimples covered her skin. Then he nibbled her ear.

She swept her long fingers over his back and down to his muscled bum cheeks, which she slowly massaged as she drew him towards her, his penis already stiffened against her belly. He kissed her eyelids, her face, her lips and the white of her throat, holding her round bottom in the palms of his hands. They continued to hold each other as they kissed each other lightly. Tingles raced across Alicia's body and down her legs.

Daniel's insides were bubbling with excitement, but he was determined to taste every part of her body. Leisurely he brushed his lips over her body, pampering her until she was wild with erotic cravings. When she let out a tiny cry and called his name, he entered her, and she pulled him in tighter and deeper with her powerful legs wrapped around his hips. She felt that she was part of him and he a part of her, their intimacy was so intense. As they gazed into each other's eyes, they were dragged into each other's inner being where thought and sense had fled.

The following few days they were both busy phoning and emailing various contacts, trying to locate Adanna's brothers. Adanna also got involved with this, as a worried

Daniel asked her questions about them and about all her relations who may have looked after them, all the time expecting her to break down. However, she grew more confident and remembered more details as the days went on, and if the rage built up again she talked it out with Alicia. She seemed to laugh more, and had reduced her hourly teeth-brushing to just a few times a day. She even forgot to pack her toothbrush in her school bag one day!

After a couple of weeks Daniel managed to track down Noah. The hospital and compound had never been re-established, as the rebels had completely demolished it the day they escaped. However, a small clinic-cum-surgery was now attached to the village orphanage, which also held a few 'hospital' beds. Noah was now working there – in fact, he was almost in charge. Tau had disappeared with his family soon after the raid and they were thought to be in Guinea.

'Hallo, my friend,' Noah's voice sung over the telephone line, and Daniel immediately felt guilty for not trying to get in touch before.

'How are you?' asked Daniel.

'Yes, well; I'm well and I now have a wife. I got married nearly a year ago.' Noah sounded very proud.

'Congratulations.'

'Yes. I am also to be a father next month.' Then, remembering Daniel's loss, he said, 'I heard about Shani. I'm sorry. How are the young ones?'

Daniel wondered how he knew about them all, and for an instant hope leapt in his heart. 'How did you know about

Shani? Did you find her … her body?' And Shani's beautiful face floated into his mind, cold and waxen.

'No. I'm afraid I did not see her after we left her with you on the shore that day.' Daniel felt his stomach twist as if he had just swallowed a stone. 'But you made some enquiries, I believe, and they filtered through to me. That was a terrible time of chaos and brutality. My father was shot and killed. My sister was kidnapped and we have only just found her; she is in very poor mental health, like Adanna was. How is she? You have her still there with you?'

'Yes; she is growing fast and doing very well at school. The war still haunts her, but she is coming along. That is why I have phoned. I need your help to find out what happened to her three brothers. And I'm extremely sorry about your father. If I can help your sister in any way you know I will.'

'That is good of you, Daniel. At the moment my sister is so traumatised we are not sure what we can do next for her. Now, give me some details about Adanna's brothers.'

'Well, firstly Adanna's real name is Anneze. We changed it because she was frightened that Commander Okafor would come and get her if he knew she was still alive.' Daniel gave Noah the details and they chatted for a further half hour. When Daniel put the phone down he felt very happy that he had called Noah. It was like catching up with ghosts; it was good to hear what had happened to the people he had grown to love at the hospital.

Later that day, when they were all sitting quietly in the lounge after dinner, Daniel placed his arm around Adanna as she sat curled up reading on the settee. 'I have something to tell you,' he said, and Adanna looked up and noticed his anxious face.

'What?' she whispered, her heart beating in her throat.

'The commander is dead. He died several days after we escaped. He was shot in the stomach and the leg and he bled to death.'

For a moment Adanna sat as still as stone; then, as if a bubble had been waiting to burst, she dropped her book and jumped up from the sofa. A huge smile came over her features and she twirled round and round with undisguised pleasure.

'Did he die quickly?' she asked suddenly, stopping her twirling and looking down at Daniel.

He was unsure how to answer, but Alicia knew. 'He had a bullet in his stomach. That would be tremendously painful and he probably took a long time to die. That sort of injury usually takes a long time to kill someone.'

Daniel shivered at Alicia's words and an image of Alicia shooting a man, standing over him, came into his mind from nowhere. He gazed at the woman he loved with a trembling heart. However, her words had a good effect on Adanna.

'Good. No more than he deserves and I hope he has gone to hell.'

'I'm sure he has,' said Alicia. She caught hold of Adanna's hand and they smiled at each other as if they had a secret. It gave Daniel the creeps.

Then a small voice said, 'I'm glad he is dead too.' Jobi slipped his podgy hand into Adanna's and stretched up as she bent down. He hugged her to him and kissed her face. Only Daniel seemed to be outside the loop, and he was at a complete loss over how he felt. The doctor in him did not accept any death easily and it was hard to see the joy it brought to others, even over a man ... no, he had not been a man. A brutal murdering rapist, who made this pure child standing in front of him, with those big earnest eyes, do things that had scarred her mind.

Rage frothed inside Daniel, and he scooped Adanna into his powerful arms and held her to his chest, love and protection for her radiating from him. She snuggled into his arms, feeling comforted and secure like she always did in his embrace. Then, after a while, Adanna and Jobi sat with Daniel as he recalled what Noah had told him about the other people they had known in the hospital. Alicia discreetly went to the kitchen and made them all hot chocolate.

Drinking the chocolate, Daniel turned to Adanna and asked, 'I've been wondering, would you like us to call you by your birth name of Anneze?'

'My passport says Adanna.'

'Yes, we could change that or just leave it, but we could still call you Anneze.'

Adanna thought for a moment. 'No, I like Adanna. It was what Shani gave me, her daughter's name, and I have become your daughter and you are my father, and I am that person now, just like the meaning of my name.'

Chapter 17

The summer turned to autumn and then to an extremely cold winter, with snow blocking the roads and turning the land into a white fairyland. Daniel decided that they should all go to Jamaica for a two week 'warm-up.' They flew into Montego Bay and were transported to their hotel, which had individual round thatched huts. They looked a bit like Adanna's hut in Africa until you went inside and saw the luxurious surroundings and enormous beds. The huts hugged the icing sugar sand, and the deep turquoise sea water was warm and clear. At night you were lulled to sleep by the breathing surf.

They all loved the sea and did some snorkelling, including Jobi who, although very young and with a prosthetic hand, could not be kept out of the water. He investigated the rocks all down one side of the beach and took photos of the different fish with the camera Alicia had bought him. He was so competent that Daniel felt able to leave him and watch him from the beach, where he and Alicia would lie, holding hands and giving each other the occasional kiss. This was a sight that Adanna had not seen yet, as they had usually had their fill of each other while she was at school, and she watched them with fascination.

One day Daniel took them on a secret trip. It turned out that he had booked for them to swim with the dolphins. That led to Jobi screeching with excitement, just like the dolphins' high-pitched babble. They all learnt to 'reggae' on the beach, Daniel and Alicia smooching each other and laughing, and Adanna and Daniel had their hair braided and Daniel cultivated a chin beard - very Jamaican.

Half way through the holiday, Adanna came out of the sea one day dripping with effervescent rainbow water that glistened on her slim, silky body. She wanted to talk to Alicia, who was sitting on the beach watching Daniel and Jobi ride on a banana boat and listening to Jobi's yells of delight as they bumped over the waves, her hand held over her deep blue eyes to block the streaming sun. Adanna flopped down next to her.

'Alicia, do you like my papa kissing you?'

Alicia turned to her, dropping her slim hand. 'Yes, otherwise I wouldn't let him do it.'

'Do you like what he does to you in bed? I sometimes hear you moan or give a little scream.'

Alicia blushed. The huts were so intimate! She looked deeply into Adanna's eyes. They were full of concern. Alicia slipped her arm round her waist and said, 'Do you think your papa would hurt me and do things I didn't like?'

Adanna hesitated, then shrugged. 'So why do you make such noises, then?' she asked.

'Oh, I think this is time for a sort of girly chat … Your papa is the tenderest of lovers. He kisses me and does pleasant things to me that give me such pleasure inside myself that little moans of rapture escape from me. Sometimes the feelings are so overwhelmingly pleasurable and *good*, that I have to express my emotion with a kind of squawk.' Alicia watched a patchwork of thoughts race across Adanna's face. Then they seemed to settle in her eyes and she whispered, 'I remember my parents loving each other like that.'

'When two people love each other, Adanna, they would never do things to each other that one does not like or enjoy. One day I hope you will find this out with a man you love.'

Adanna shook her braided head and seemed to shrink. 'Never. I do not ever want a man – ever.'

'Not even if he is like your papa?'

Adanna looked bewildered. Big shiny tears glistened in the corners of her eyes.

'I felt like you once. My heart was frozen, especially against men. I know I have never been raped and abused like you – and not just from the commander – but the men who raped you were not the type of men that anyone would or could fall in love with.'

'Some were just boys and some were husbands and fathers.' Adanna's big eyes were now streaming with large tears that rolled over her cheeks.

'Yes, but didn't you tell me that they were on drugs? Even the young boys were cut deliberately and had drugs rubbed into their cuts to make them able to kill and do the things they did. Do you think that your brothers would ever do such things to a female?'

'No.' Then Adanna added, 'Not unless they were drugged; it made all the boys go crackers and, like you said, do terrible things.'

'Yes. That's right. In a way those boys were abused too. They will never be the same.'

'I remember one of the boys one night after they had been on a raid. The drug had nearly worn off. He suddenly got up and shot himself through the head … Dead.' And Adanna shivered at the memory. 'After that, the commander would take all the guns and weapons from the returning young soldiers and keep them locked away.'

'So you see that not all men are like the commander. He was evil and very sick. One day I am convinced you will find a good man and you will want him to love you, and he will be very caring, like your papa. You will want to love him because you won't be able to help yourself.'

'Like you.'

'Yes. I cannot help but love your papa with all my heart.'

'But how can any man love me after what has happened to me?'

'They will, just like your papa loves me even though I have had a bad past. When you fall in love it is not logical. Feelings come over you that you are too weak to resist. Love hits you like a virus. It will happen to you, you'll see. But there is plenty of time; get that career you are after first and then, when you least expect it, boom, it will happen. You will be so much in love, because you are a person who gives out love and warmth.'

However, Adanna still thought that she would never, ever, want to have sex with anyone again. To her it was not a loving experience, and it was beyond her comprehension that it ever could be. True, she had learnt to love again – her papa, Jobi and now Alicia – and have emotions again, even happy emotions sometimes. No, it was off her list; but if what Alicia said was true then … OK. It seemed that she would be unable to stop herself. But the thought of being with anyone in that way again scared her. Memories of the rapes with the commander were still so strong. She had been his 'bush wife', and not only had she been raped each night by him, she had also endured, sometimes all night, being raped by the 'young virgin boys' that the commander insisted she 'helped'. They would take their turns until she just lay there, not even protesting anymore, letting them do what they liked as if she was a ragged doll.

She got used to being raped and her mind turned to blank stone. Even the thought of escaping or killing herself disappeared, although from the start she had been locked up naked in a bare room with the other girls and kept an eye on so that escape or suicide were impossible. Suddenly, feelings of being trapped and helpless came dashing headlong into her frothing stomach like a great express train, roaring and flashing, and vomit threatened to race up her throat. She grabbed her stomach and, no longer seeing the beautiful sparkling sea in front of her, rushed up the powdery sand into the darkness of the hut, where she washed herself vigorously under the shower before brushing her teeth with such ferocity that it was a wonder her teeth stayed in their sockets.

For the first time Alicia felt powerless to help Adanna. Alicia herself was so dizzy with love that she felt like a cloud drifting across the bluest of skies. She woke almost every morning now having had a sound sleep and no bad dreams, laughter like that of a new-born baby bubbling out of her. At this moment she wished and prayed that some of her warm, happy emotions could be transferred to Adanna.

Alicia had at last learnt a trick, with Daniel's help, to counteract any bad dreams or thoughts that tried to enter her mind with a good thought, and most times it worked. As the days went on she recalled more and more happier memories of her family and blocked out the bad recollections of what had happened and what she had done.

Slowly, she strolled towards the hut after Adanna, thinking hard. She knew that there was no hurry; that Adanna would go through the ritual of washing and scrubbing. She felt swamped, but guilty about feeling so happy while Adanna was so sad. Adanna was like a glowing star that had lost her way, just like she had before Daniel. Alicia was sure Adanna had been a star before the war; she saw glimpses of it occasionally, when she teased her father or Jobi and when she sang or played music on the piano which Daniel had bought soon after they had moved from London. Sometimes Alicia would accompany her, doubling up with laughter as they tried to race each other over the keys to a piece of music. This also brought back reminders to Alicia about her life in Devon and playing music with her dad.

Alicia had known that Adanna's questions would come. She had seen her staring at her and Daniel when they kissed. Daniel thought it would be good for Adanna to see how loving a relationship could be, and he had refused to stop displaying affection or kissing Alicia in front of her. They hadn't thought about their lovemaking. Now look what had happened. Also Alicia had noticed that, the previous evening, Adanna had hurried back from getting herself an ice cream from the restaurant after a young man had tried to speak to her. After that, she had hardly moved from their side all night.

When Adanna came out of the shower, Alicia decided to give her a challenge and take her sailing. There were sailing boats for hire on the beach and Alicia had booked one.

'Put on your bikini, we are going sailing, kiddo. I'll show you how to do it. It's not easy until you get the hang of it.' As a child Alicia had done lots of sailing with her brother and dad and loved it. It made her feel free and relaxed, and she hoped it would do the same for Adanna. She knew that sitting around giving Adanna time for more devastating thoughts to submerge her mind would not help. Learning a new skill left no room for other thoughts, and besides, sailing was exciting.

After a couple of hours Adanna struggled up the beach, smiling like a sunbeam, her hair drenched and sparkling with salt crystals. She had learnt to sail and she thought it was wonderful. She could not wait to do it again. When Jobi rushed at her and hung onto her arm she scooped him up and together they all planned to go sailing the next day.

'I'll teach you how to sail, Papa,' grinned Adanna. She would take him into the choppy sea just off the rocks like Alicia did. It had made Adanna's tummy jump as they dipped and tossed and, because she was a beginner, she had wondered if she would survive or drown. It had been a challenge to her mood and Alicia had known it. Adanna did not want to die; she realised that there was too much to live for and enjoy … Even without a man.

On the last day before they were due to fly home they all climbed the Dunn falls, as legend says that if you get to the top you will come back to Jamaica. They all wanted to come back. Adanna even wanted them to live there. 'It is like England with sunshine,' she declared, 'but people here have happy faces and are so happy. It reminds me of being in Africa before the fighting, and our skin colour is not out of place here either.'

'Mine is, and your papa's sort of,' chuckled Alicia.

Daniel placed his arm around Adanna's shoulders and kissed her soft cheek. 'We will come again soon,' he promised, 'as a treat after your exams.'

Chapter 18

When they got back to England there were several calls for Daniel on the answerphone. There was news about Adanna's brothers. The eldest brother, Mosi, who was now nearly twenty-two, and the youngest brother, Eban, who had just turned ten, had been found living in a rock quarry. They had been traced by looking in their relatives' villages. It was discovered that they had been living with their mother's brother, their Uncle Imari, in his village for several years. Unfortunately, Uncle Imari was not strong due to injuries from the war and, with very little food, had caught an infection and died.

The boys were then traced via some villagers who knew that they were now living in a plastic shelter at the quarry in Freetown, where they both worked breaking up rocks. That was why it had taken six months to find them. The information had come the day after they had left for their holiday, so Daniel rang immediately and was told that the middle boy, Nuru, who would have been eighteen, had died from taking drugs and not eating properly. He had been captured a few weeks after Adanna had been kidnapped, and had become a child soldier. Although taken in by his uncle after the war, they could not help him to come off the drugs, and he would steal to get money. He had lived half with them and half in the slums of Freetown.

Daniel started questioning the cold voice on the other end of the phone like an inquisitor, trying to discover how he could get in touch with Mosi, the eldest boy. He heard the icy voice snigger, which made his blood boil. It had been like this when he made enquiries about Shani. The voice did not suggest anything helpful. He was told that he could not write or phone, as the boys had no house to send a letter or make a phone call to. When Daniel suggested that the boys could surely use the telephone to which he was speaking right now, he was 'educated' in the logistics of such a task. Exasperated, he asked for the address of the quarry. Maybe he could ask Noah to go and find the boys, bring them back with him and take them to a telephone so that Daniel and Adanna could at least speak to them.

Noah and Daniel were in touch most weeks. Noah had had a baby boy and enlightened Daniel on the baby's progress each time he phoned, his pride in his son shining down the telephone line. It reminded Daniel of how he had felt about his son before he died, and he decided to ask Alicia if she was ready to give him a child. They had been together now for nearly two years.

Daniel had ordered medicines and several computers for Noah's clinic, and Noah had learnt to email. Daniel had also managed to find and fund a counsellor for Noah's sister Charity, which had been a success not only for her but for other girls too. Noah had set up regular sessions, which had succeeded in giving the girls back their pride so that they were able to motivate themselves again. Charity, having had an education before her marriage and the war, was teaching in the expanding orphanage that Alicia was funding. The building was being renovated and new rooms added, using the money from the sale of Alicia's house.

When Daniel asked for Noah's help for the boys, Noah said that he would set out the next morning to fetch them. True to his word, three days later a phone call came through that brought such a radiance to Adanna's face that Daniel was unable to hold back his tears.

At first Mosi could not believe it was his sister he was talking to because he had heard she had died, but Noah told him about the 'swap' at the hospital and, after speaking to Adanna for ten minutes, he broke down in tears as he realised she was indeed his sister. Several weeks later Adanna and her brothers were speaking to each other every day, running up huge phone bills for both the orphanage and Daniel until he discovered that Mosi could read and write. Charity and Noah taught him how to email, so Adanna was always on the computer, emailing every day and phoning twice a week.

Daniel had also arranged for the boys to stay at Noah's orphanage, even though Mosi was too old to be there. They assigned Mosi a job helping to paint the walls of the orphanage and the new rooms of the clinic, and he found that his skill for painting extended to fantastic animal murals. He did several for Charity's schoolroom, and later he painted the children's dormitories. Animals peeped from bushes; lions lounged under trees or prowled around the African desert, and creeping snakes curled up in cool grass under a burning sun. Alongside each animal was its name in black paint.

Daniel also had long conversations with Mosi, and asked him if he would like to come to England, but Mosi was adamant that he wished to stay in Africa. However, when Adanna told him about the exams she was taking and that she was going to be a doctor, Mosi said that he would like help to continue his education and maybe make something of himself.

As he was the first-born he had had the privilege of going to school until the war. So, with Noah's help, Daniel found a college for Mosi to go to, and Charity helped him with extra lessons before he started. Eban was now going to the orphanage school. He was supposed to sleep in one of the boys' dormitories but he hated being parted from Mosi at night, so he would go to Mosi's cupboard room and snuggle on the shelf with him. Meanwhile, Daniel was in negotiations to buy a new three-bedroomed bungalow on a gated estate a mile from the orphanage. It was intended for the boys, but when he found out how cheap they were he bought another for Noah to live in. But Noah insisted on paying rent before he would agree to live there.

The change in Adanna was astonishing. She laughed more, had more energy and was totally committed to becoming a doctor. When not doing homework or talking to her brothers she would pore over the internet, learning as much as she could about symptoms and diseases, which she would discuss very knowledgably with Daniel.

Early one Saturday morning she stunned Daniel by announcing that she had made arrangements to join the local Red Cross and help out at their shop in town. She also informed him that she was quite capable of getting there by herself by bus – and off she went. Daniel hadn't been aware that she even knew there were buses from the village to town!

And that was just the beginning of Adanna's growing independence. When she finished her exams that summer, Daniel asked her if she wished to visit her brothers.

'There is no way I am going back to Sierra Leone,' she replied, then added in a small quivering voice, her face collapsed like a pricked balloon, 'Do you want to send me back there?'

Daniel shook his head and put his arm around her drooping shoulders. 'Maybe I could arrange for your brothers to go to Jamaica and meet us for a holiday, then.' Adanna's eyes filled with tears and she twisted, throwing herself into his arms.

'I promise that one day, somehow, I will pay you back.'

Daniel dropped his smile. 'You are my daughter, you give me such pleasure; you owe me nothing, and certainly not money.'

Several weeks later, Adanna hopped from foot to foot as she waited at the airport arrival gate. The family had been in Jamaica for two days. Daniel had wanted to rent a large house as they were staying for a month, but Adanna and Jobi wanted to go back to the hotel they had stayed at before, as Adanna said, there was so much entertainment for the children, Jobi and Eban to enjoy. It seemed that Adanna was no longer a child. She had gone into 'Mother' mode, which amused Daniel no end.

When Adanna and her brothers came face to face with each other they cried and hugged. It took nearly two days before the three of them stopped weeping each time they gazed at each other. The boys were overwhelmed by the huts, the food and the surroundings, and told Daniel they felt like royalty. Jobi and Eban hit it off together and were soon inseparable, even choosing to eat the same food.

Daniel and Alicia got on well with Mosi and after a week declared him a very nice young man. He was respectful, polite and sensible. He also adored dancing, and, as Adanna's protector, helped her to join in the dancing and entertainment. At one point she was in stitches of laughter and could not stand up! Each evening she would rush to get dressed up and ask Alicia to help with her hair.

After a week Mosi and Adanna sat talking and crying together on the beach, opening up to each other about their war experiences. When Mosi heard what Adanna had been through, tears like pearl drops rolled over his cheeks unheeded. Towards the end of the holiday Mosi, again with tears glistening in the corners of his eyes, thanked Daniel for rescuing his sister and looking after her so well. He said that he would be eternally grateful for all Daniel had done for her, his brother and himself.

'You have breathed new life into my family and I will never let you down. I will prove worthy of your concern.'

Mosi sobbed when they parted at the airport. Adanna and Jobi were too distraught to say much at all.

'We will see you again; maybe here in the winter – well, England's winter – but definitely sometime in the New Year,' Daniel assured them all.

Chapter 19

Adanna finding her brothers was both a happy and a sad time for Alicia. She was happy for Adanna, but it brought back her nightmares about her brother's and sister-in-law's deaths – and, most of all, the rage that had slipped from her heart and mind when she had first moved in with Daniel. She constantly saw her brother's pale and bloody face as he died in her arms, and some nights she awoke with perspiration soaking her body. Daniel would hold her damp, naked body against his and stroke her hair, asking her questions about her childhood until she recalled some happy images.

Daniel found it wearing. Adanna was happy, but now he had Alicia to deal with. When they reached Jamaica, the day before Adanna's brothers were due to fly in he had suggested that she should stay with Jobi while he went to the airport with Adanna, frightened that she may break down in the face of the bad memories – it could have been her brother, if only … However, Alicia suddenly seemed to turn a corner a few days into the holiday, like a wilting flower put into a vase of water. She got her smile back and slept peacefully at night.

'I was wondering how you felt about us having a child soon,' Daniel asked, one night towards the end of their holiday. He had been longing to ask her, but because of her dreams he had felt unable to talk about it earlier.

'Mmm. I would love your child, Daniel. I want my own family. I love yours, but I would love to have my own child.'

'Yes, I feel the same.'

Alicia threw Daniel her sunbeam smile and watched his deep brown eyes fill with a mischievous light. He gave her his lopsided boyish grin.

'I shall stop taking the pill from tomorrow, then,' she said as Daniel drew her into his arms.

Back in England they all settled down to the coming winter, which seemed to be arriving early. The bitter chill ate into their bones at night. Adanna had passed all her exams with flying colours and had joined the Red Cross as a first aider on some of their jaunts. She went to events like horse trials, football matches and motorbike scrambling to put some of her theory into practice. It reminded her of the things that Shani had let her do back in the compound, and how she had enjoyed every moment. She became even more determined to become a doctor.

It was nearly a year since Daniel had registered Shani's sons with the refugee agency and the Red Cross. He still kept phoning every week, but there was no news and he seemed no closer to finding them than when he started. Alicia had also tried; she tried every refugee agency that she worked with and some she didn't, but still no news. One evening, while Daniel was out with Jobi at his junior chess club, Alicia saw a programme on TV about refugee boys who had come to Manchester from Sierra Leone several years ago. The programme was following several of the boys, now young men, on their progress, finding out how they had settled into Britain. She took down the name of the project and told Daniel about it that night. The following day she sent an email with the details of Shani's sons.

Alicia had had three periods since their return from Jamaica. Each month, eyes shining with tears, she had told Daniel that she was not pregnant. He was disappointed, but he didn't let it show.

'These things can take time, especially after taking the pill,' and he added with a grin, 'Maybe we should practise more.'

'Practise more!' Alicia said, wide-eyed. 'That would mean never getting out of bed, then.'

'It will happen, you'll see.' Daniel drew her into his strong arms, holding her gently. 'After all, you are not quite thirty yet; plenty of time. I wasn't going to tell you yet, but to cheer you up I have a surprise for your birthday next week … well, in a couple of weeks' time. Just after your birthday, actually. You know I have to go to a one-day medical conference in Brighton on the Saturday; well, I have arranged for my mum and dad to have the children for a long weekend so that you can come too. I've booked a luxurious suite from Friday to Monday. On the Friday we can get pampered in the spa, and in the evening I have booked us tickets to see an ice ballet of *Swan Lake*. On the Saturday you can go shopping while I go to the conference, and on Sunday I've booked a hot air balloon trip. You've always said you wanted a ride in one of them! They are having some sort of balloon day – about half a dozen balloons, I think.'

Alicia gazed up into Daniel's brown eyes. They were so full of warmth. She wanted his child more than ever – with just the same eyes.

'Well ...'

'I love you.' Alicia, reaching up, pressed her lips to Daniel's mouth.

Daniel, his tackle at the ready whenever Alicia was near, drew her down onto his lap as he collapsed on the sofa. 'It will happen, I promise,' he said huskily, as he traced her neck with his tongue. Then, with his finger under her chin, he buried his tongue between her lips. Their tongues danced wildly as they both got hot and bothered.

'Dad,' Jobi said, pulling at Daniel's shirt sleeve and standing dripping with water, a long white towel over his head making him look like a hooded ghost. 'You forgot me!'

Daniel broke away from Alicia and stared at his young son. Jobi was glistening with soap bubbles that were slowly sliding over his nut-brown skin and down his legs, landing up in a wet pool of rainbow globules on the sitting room carpet.

Alicia tried to smother a laugh as Daniel's lips went tight.

'How much of the bottle of bubble bath have you used?'

'All of it!' Jobi answered honestly. 'They are everywhere and ...'

'I can see that,' broke in Daniel.

'They are beautiful, like magic,' Jobi whispered to Alicia. 'They are up the wall and over the floor and the sun is shining on them and they turn to all different colours,' he finished triumphantly.

Daniel groaned, tipping Alicia off his lap as he stood up. 'Sunday mornings.' He shook his head. 'And I had not forgotten you. I just came down to get my coffee and got waylaid.'

'What's waylaid?'

'Yes,' Alicia asked, smirking. 'What exactly do you mean by waylaid?'

'Oooooooh!' Daniel shouted. He grabbed Jobi's towel from his head, swiftly wrapped it around his skinny body and swept him up into the air, where he let out giggles as Daniel raced him up the stairs in his arms.

Alicia, going to get another towel from the hall cupboard to help dry the puddle, grinned to herself as she heard Daniel let out a deep growl when he saw the state of the bathroom.

Chapter 20

Alicia opened the front door and Jobi flung himself at her, smiling like a Cheshire cat and holding a Jobi-wrapped present (lots of sticky tape and paper not meeting over the article). Alicia, trying to stay upright and balance herself, burst into bubbly laughter.

'Happy birthday!' yelled Jobi.

'Wow, Jobi; this looks exciting,' Alicia said, untangling herself from his long, spidery arms. Turning, she placed her office bag on the hall floor and undid her jacket.

'Let Alicia get in,' said Adanna, her eyes rolling at Jobi's exuberance.

'Open it, open it. I made it myself,' and he started to open the parcel.

Adanna snatched it away from his nimble fingers. 'It's Alicia's birthday present; let her open it.'

'I was only helping.'

Daniel, grinning widely, came into the hall and winked at Alicia. 'Bring Alicia into the kitchen and we shall have tea. She can open the presents there, Jobi.'

Jobi grabbed Alicia's hand, dragging her from the hall into the family kitchen.

'Hi.' Alicia smiled, and managed to kiss Daniel as she wandered past. Entering the kitchen, she saw a beautiful *red* cake with rainbow-coloured sprinkles and candles on the dining table.

'I chose the colours and decorated it,' said Jobi, jumping up and down.

'Well, I have to say I have truly never had such a wonderful-looking cake ever.'

'And I made the cake – chocolate,' said Adanna.

'Mmm, yummy. My favourite flavour from the world's best cake cook.' Alicia turned to Daniel, who smirked.

'And I made the tea; Earl Grey. Kindly sit,' and Daniel pulled out her chair.

'Open my present first,' said Jobi, thrusting it into Alicia's hands as she took a seat and settled down.

'Here.' Daniel handed her a pair of scissors and Alicia wriggled in her seat, pretending to be excited with the mystery of unwrapping the parcel, although she could already see that it was a clay pot highly decorated with glass beads.

'Oh Jobi. It is absolutely beautiful; you sure you made this?'

Jobi nodded seriously. 'I got the clay with Dad a couple of weeks ago. It dries in the air, so I hid it in the garage so you didn't discover it.'

'I shall keep my earrings in it on my dressing table, and when the sun hits the beads they will glisten. Oh, I love it, Jobi. Thank you,' and she hugged Jobi and pulled him onto her lap, where he squirmed with happiness and twined his arms around her neck.

'Here's mine,' said Adanna, wanting to jump up and down but refrained; after all, she was seventeen now and it was not ladylike.

Alicia, with Jobi's help, undid the pretty pink paper. The present was a blue chiffon top that Alicia had seen and wanted, but the shop had not had her size in stock. 'Oh, Adanna, you got the top! It's so delicate and lovely. Thank you.' Alicia held it against her as Jobi slipped his arms away.

'I went in and ordered your size the next day.'

Alicia bent forward and kissed her. 'Thanks. I shall wear it tonight when Dad takes me out.'

'And my present is going to wait until tonight,' Daniel said.

'I thought we were going to Brighton in a couple of weeks for my birthday present from you.'

'That too, but I have something for you today too.'

Adanna and Daniel exchanged glances and Jobi said, 'You will want to …'

Daniel and Adanna shouted together for Jobi to be quiet.

'I wasn't …'

Daniel broke in, 'Let's light the candles, shall we?' and took a box of matches from the kitchen drawer.

Three hours later Alicia gave a twirl to her audience; she was wearing the floaty blue top that hung low in delicate folds across the smooth skin of her breasts and turned her eyes into deep blue pools. She wore it over a short, tight, black skirt that clung to the curve of her hips and accentuated her long legs. Daniel found his trousers doing their usual tighten trick and wished he was taking her to bed instead of taking her to dinner.

'Gorgeous,' he said huskily, and Alicia threw him a mischievous grin and swayed her hips from side to side as she turned, very slowly, in a kind of sexy dance.

They had dinner in a restaurant overlooking the harbour, which was edged with twinkling lights like lost Atlantis. The dinner had been superb, and they sat back in their wicker chairs full and relaxed.

'My present,' Daniel said, and extracted a small grey velvet box from his pocket.

Alicia glanced down at the tiny box and her stomach did a somersault. Was he …? Did he …? Daniel opened the box and took her slim hand. Two diamonds on a twist sparkled at her.

'I thought the ring represented two lovers entwined. Will you marry me, please?'

Alicia swallowed. Her eyes filled with tears. She nodded, and the tears fell from her eyes like a mountain torrent and rolled down her cheeks.

Daniel stared at her for a moment, then jokingly said, 'If I'd thought marrying me would make you cry, maybe I shouldn't have asked. It is supposed to make you feel happy.'

'Oh, I am happy, and I feel *very* loved. Oh, I love you so much.' And love shook like a windy reed in her heart. Through a mist of tears she sought her bag, found a tissue and wiped her eyes. Daniel, looking completely lost, took the tissue from her and dabbed at the tears on her soft cheeks; then, bending close to her, he kissed her wet cheeks until she laughed and kissed him back. He slipped the ring onto her finger.

After they had got home and said goodnight to Mrs Jones, they crept upstairs to bed, kissing each other hungrily. The two children came bursting out of their bedrooms, Jobi practically wagging his tail like Squirt had done five minutes earlier.

'Well, what was the answer?' Adanna asked.

Daniel just nodded at them. They both threw themselves at Alicia with high-pitched squeals.

Chapter 21

Alicia stretched her slim body under the sheet like a cat. Turning, she felt the warm spot that Daniel had just vacated and she snuggled down into the warm hole that smelt of him. She was so happy; she felt sure she was pregnant after yesterday. They had made love several times, once in the afternoon after they had been to the spa and again after the ballet and supper.

The hotel suite was opulent, with cream walls, green and gold silk curtains, and velvet chairs in the sitting room. The theme continued in the bedroom, with soft lighting, an enormous bed covered with a cream silk bedspread edged in green and gold, and matching accessories. When they arrived, the bed was covered with red rose petals, and in the middle was a white swan made from towels. They were just in time for lunch. Afterwards they went for a swim in the giant pool, and later they each had a full body massage. When they returned to their suite they felt utterly relaxed.

'If I don't get pregnant feeling so relaxed, I never will,' Alicia had said as she lay spread-eagled on the silky cream cover, her body smothered in the rose petals that Daniel had picked up and sprinkled over her. 'But I'm not sure I've got any energy.'

Daniel slipped his warm, wet lips over her belly. 'Looks like I will have to help myself – if you don't mind, that is,' he said, gazing up with his lopsided grin.

Alicia giggled. 'Oh do, do help yourself.'

And he had tasted every part of her and fondled her body with expert fingers, sending shivers through her and making her squirm with sexual arousal, her body heightened to his every touch. When he entered her, their passion grew and he exploded. Alicia felt sure that she felt his sperm swimming towards a new life inside her.

Daniel, coming out of the bathroom threw his damp body onto the bed next to her as she huddled under the covers. 'What are you smiling about?'

'I'm sure I'm pregnant after last night; such a lovely birthday present,' and she slipped her arms around Daniel's neck as he chuckled at her.

He kissed the top of her head and shifted off the bed, opening the wardrobe and removing a crisp white shirt. 'We shall see, but we had still better keep practising.'

'Now, if you want,' Alicia said, kicking off the bed covers, lying tantalisingly naked and grinning like an enchanted fairy.

'Oh, don't,' Daniel groaned. 'I'm already going to be late. What are you planning to do today?'

Alicia spun from the bed and, giggling, glided over to Daniel, who was trying to put his trousers on. She clasped him around the stomach, pressed herself up against his backside and slithered her hand around to his manhood, which he was trying with some difficulty to pack into his trousers.

'You little witch.'

Alicia, now curled up with laughter, floated to the bathroom as Daniel made a grab for her but missed. 'You haven't got time, remember,' she said, and vanished from his sight. He heard the running of the taps as he tucked in his shirt and glided a tie around his neck. *Gosh, that woman has such power over me.*

'What time does your conference finish?' asked Alicia, coming back into the room with a towel wrapped around her. It was a small towel, and her sexy body and long legs had Daniel all hot again.

He inhaled deeply and turned his back to Alicia, ruffling his jacket from the coat hook in the wardrobe. He would have to put it on just before he entered the conference room; he felt as hot as the hinges of hell just looking at Alicia.

'About five. I'll meet you down in the tea room and then later we are all having dinner at eight, which you are invited to.' He strode over to Alicia and kissed her lightly.

'Is that supposed to last me all day?' she pouted.

Daniel whimpered like an injured animal, took her in his arms and planted his warm lips on hers. She opened her mouth and sought his tongue. He dropped his jacket, feeling her naked breasts against his cotton shirt. The small towel had already unwrapped itself and fallen to the floor. He was as hard as a rock and Alicia knew it. She teased him by drifting her hands to his backside and holding him tightly to her. She adored the dominance she had over him. Each time she tested it he utterly succumbed.

'Well, you had better go; my bath is nearly ready. Enjoy your day,' and, smirking like a cat that had just caught a tasty mouse, she picked up her towel and his jacket from the floor. She handed Daniel the jacket and disappeared into the bathroom.

Racing down the stairs, Daniel shook himself out of his sexual daze and thought about how Alicia had changed from a shy, hesitant virgin to a confident sexual temptress. He loved every moment of it.

Chapter 22

Daniel and Alicia were seated in the hotel tea room scoffing scones and cream with a Doctor Penny Reynalds, her husband, and a Doctor Moore. Suddenly Alicia, in the middle of telling Daniel about a dress she had bought for Adanna stopped dead and looked up as Doctor Moore stood up. She went as white as chalk, her pallid cheeks emphasising her swirling blue eyes. She began to heave and Penny, who was seated opposite her, asked if she was OK just as Alicia vomited across the table. Doctor Moore was now holding out his hand to a tall, robust man with sable hair and deep-set ferret eyes.

'May I introduce Doctor Zerac, an obstetrician from Thailand whom I admire greatly ... Oh, are you ill, Alicia?'

Daniel jumped to his feet when Alicia vomited and put an arm around her shoulders. She was trembling like a frightened child. It was a moment before the stranger's name sunk in and Daniel realised who he was. 'Sorry,' he said, lifting Alicia to her feet. 'She ... she's eaten too much cream.'

Members of staff had appeared immediately like bees around a honey pot. They removed the tablecloth, sprayed the table with disinfectant and covered it with a fresh white tablecloth all in the blink of an eye.

'Can we get you anything?' the concerned manager asked. Alicia managed to shake her head.

Daniel half carried Alicia away from the table. 'I will take her upstairs ... Let her have a sleep.'

Zerac's face swam into focus as Alicia stared at him. He was smiling down at her, his features radiant with victory.

'Oh, I'm sorry you are not well, but I'm sure you will soon feel better. We shall see each other later at dinner tonight, perhaps, or tomorrow. I understand we are all going ballooning,' Zerac smirked.

'Not me,' said Doctor Moore. 'Can't stand heights, let alone being in one of those balloon jobbies,' and the buzz of conversation drifted away as Daniel and Alicia went through the lobby towards the lift. Alicia was clammy, her pale lemon dress clinging to her like a lettuce leaf.

'I need air, not our room,' she said. An odd tone had entered her voice, and Daniel guided her out into the hotel grounds and sat her down on the nearest bench. She shook herself free of Daniel's arm, letting the slight breeze catch at her damp hair, lifting it and whispering her name. It was her dead relatives calling her … then she realised it was Daniel. She needed to be alone, to gather her thoughts; she knew Daniel would start questioning her. She shivered. The breeze had done its work and her body was dry with the cold.

'Can you go and get my coat, please?'

Daniel nodded. 'You sure you will be alright if I leave you?'

'I'll be fine, but I need my coat.'

Daniel rushed across the lawn and raced up the stairs like a hare. What was going to happen now? Maybe the police! Would they be interested in what this man did in another country? Interpol, then. Would that mean that Alicia's …. Maybe he should suggest it to Alicia first after he took her away as quickly as he could from this hotel and that man. He feared what she might do. Where was her damn coat?

Out in the gardens Alicia gazed unseeingly at the flowers around her. It had been such a shock; she had never expected to meet him again. Her stomach was churning like she had swallowed a tornado and the taste of vomit was acid on her tongue. Suddenly, Zerac was beside her. She twisted round and stared up at him as he observed her in silence.

'Well, you have turned into a beautiful young woman. I understand that the concerned, loving doctor is your fiancé.' He sat down casually on the wooden bench and leaned into her. 'I looked for you when I found out you were still alive, but I only found that out a few years ago when I went back home to Slovenia. I live in Thailand now and always half did; I had a second family there that my other family knew nothing about. My Slovenian family all died in the war, just like yours.' Zerac kept his voice low while Alicia sat pale and grave as if she was a sculptured stone.

He went on crisply, his sunglasses perched on top of his head catching the last of the evening sunlight like two menacing snake's eyes, 'I was going to give you a nasty ending, just like your parents, in case you try to say something to the authorities about what I did … Mmm, actually, now I have seen you again, I've decided I want you. You can be one of my mistresses. I'll take you back to Thailand and settle you in my … harem.' He sniggered. 'At least for a while …'

'In your dreams.' Alicia's voice wobbled.

'Yes; now I've seen you, I will dream of you all night.' He chuckled looking Alicia up and down. 'Yes, I'm going to enjoy you – and if you don't comply, I will have people kill your new family. I might even do it myself. Although, come to think of it, I might just leave the girl, Adanna isn't it, I think that is what Doctor Moore called her – about seventeen? – and use her in my baby farm. The choice is yours.' Choice! He threw back his head crackling with laughter. 'I want your answer by Monday morning. We can go home together, won't that be nice – and don't think of mentioning this to anyone. My power has a long reach and you know what I am capable of. See you tonight at dinner, my sweet thing,' and he placed his large paw under Alicia's chin and turned her face to look at him. Her eyes were filled with hate, which seemed only to amuse Zerac. 'Oh, I'm going to be entertained with you.'

When Daniel arrived there was no sign of Zerac. He had strolled back into the hotel as though he owned the place, turning and winking at Alicia while grinning like a demented cat.

'Your coat was in the car. Sorry I was so long.' Daniel slipped the coat around Alicia's shoulders. 'Are you feeling better?' Then, realising what a silly thing he had just said, he slumped onto the garden bench. 'Sorry. I don't know what I can do for you. Sorry.'

Alicia shot up from the bench. 'Stop saying sorry, and there is nothing you can do. I want a bath. I suddenly feel dirty,' and she marched into the hotel with Daniel following, his heart as heavy as Alicia's if only she had known it.

Chapter 23

'Well, crack open that champagne then,' said Petrov Zerac, a smug smile on his face, as the balloon began to drift into the air. He stuffed his hip flask into his pocket and lit his cigar, sucking on it and inhaling deeply as he leant casually against the side of the basket, holding onto the balloon rope. The burner crackled above Alicia's head through the ring of cigar smoke.

Where were the pilot and the others? How had Zerac managed to partner just her in the balloon? Somehow she had known that he would wangle a trip with her and Daniel, so she had left Daniel safe, drugged in bed. A worm of fear wriggled in her stomach as she tried not to show how scared she was. Why, oh why, did she feel so frightened? She knew the answer; she wanted to live, not die. To live her life with Daniel and his love. Now her life mattered, but Zerac had threatened her new family. She knew that even if she gave in to his demands he would still kill them. How was she going to stop him?

'This is going to be fun, I can tell,' Zerac smirked; then, bending towards her, he whispered intimately, 'Being just the two of us, I can have an early taste of you,' and with that he pulled the cord so that the balloon discharged an explosion of gas, shooting higher into the shimmering morning sky away from the other five balloons. Alicia seesawed, clinging with one hand to the basket side and holding the bottle of champagne in the other hand.

Zerac then asked, 'What did you do with Doc Daniel? I had plans for him,' and he threw back his head and began to chortle. To Alicia it resembled the hiss of a serpent. 'I thought I would topple him into the sea.' He gave Alicia the same smile that he had had on his face after he had shot her parents, a smile of triumph as if he had won some gold Olympic medal, but this time his eyes blazed like deep forests of desire. Suddenly she felt as vulnerable as the schoolgirl she had been on that horrific day on her parents' stairs.

She was tougher now?... And she tried to smile back.

'The champagne.' Zerac nodded towards the bottle, leaning against the side of the basket. Obeying, Alicia levered the top of the champagne off, her hands trembling. As the cork shot from the bottle like a bullet, the bubbling fizz burst into the air over her slim hands and splashed across her blouse. Startled, she overbalanced and swayed onto the floor of the basket. Looking up at Zerac, she knew he had noticed how scared she was; his expression leapt to power and he stepped forward and tugged at her blouse until the buttons popped off.

'Save undoing them and easier for me to lick the champagne off your breasts.'

Anger came roaring like billows on an unseen shore, their fury sweeping over Alicia, and hate darkened her soul. 'I prefer mine in a glass,' she said, standing up and holding out the bottle, now with a steady hand.

Zerac arched his eyebrows and, turning his back, reached for the champagne flutes that were in a bag hanging from the basket's side. Madness clouded Alicia's mind like black shapes. She stepped swiftly towards him and hit him on the back of the head with the champagne bottle. All her pent-up, hungry hostility gave her arm the strength of steel and the bottle smashed into pieces, sending sparkling silvery wings of liquid through Zerac's thick black hair.

Zerac staggered, stunned, then his knees buckled and, still holding the crystal glasses, he fell onto the floor of the balloon basket. The cigar dropped from his mouth and rolled onto his silk shirt. Alicia, quivering like jelly, backed out of his reach and stood rigidly against the far side of the tiny basket.

'You little bitch,' Zerac hissed, blood oozing in silent rivers from the side of his head. He let the glasses fall and they rotated towards Alicia, clinking together like dainty wind chimes, *just like the garden chime I had when I was a child*. She stood as cold as an iceberg with hot tears of rage streaming down her face as she watched Zerac swaying and scrambling to get to his feet. Pitching forward, he grabbed Alicia's left leg and started to drag himself up, unbalancing her. She slipped on the wet slimy floor and fell down. Then Zerac flung himself at her like a mad bull. He pinned her throat with his large hand, pushing her backwards against the woven side.

Laughing loudly, he said, 'Well, my little hellcat, I will soon have you tamed,' and with his free hand he yanked at Alicia's lace bra, which was showing through her gaping blouse. 'Just look at those beautiful plump breasts just ripe for a lick.'

Alicia stiffened as Zerac bent towards her. The fingers of her right hand were still curled around the jagged bottleneck and, as Zerac gazed at her exposed breasts, she instinctively thrust the bottle into the soft flesh of his face. It sunk in like a knife cutting into a melon, making her shudder, but psychotic rage had engulfed her. As he let out a guttural holler she twisted the barbed edges with all her strength, mashing them into soft tissue, her teeth clenched. She wrestled to keep the bottle in place as Zerac wildly tried to grasp her arms. Thick red blood spurted over her hand and face like a fountain. It trickled down her body, warm, wet and smelling just like the memory of her other 'assassinations'. It all spun in her mind like a spider's web. With the saw-toothed glass planted deep in the muscles of his face, Zerac was slowly going limp, and at last he sunk to the floor like a packet of crumbling biscuits. Alicia, with a smile playing around her lips, tugged the fractured remains of the bottle from his face. An unearthly scream of pain, like the sound that Michelle made before she died, was rent from Zerac's mouth, and he fell backwards against the basket side holding his gored face between his two bloody hands. One eyeball, like a child's Halloween sweet, hung on the jagged edge of the broken bottle. Alicia stared at it uncomprehendingly.

The balloon had soared swiftly up into the clouds after Zerac had pulled the cord, crossing the land, catching the wind, but now it was dipping over the grey English Channel, hitting the water occasionally, then flying into the air again for a minute at a time. Alicia absorbed the bumps like a drunken sailor as she quivered, hearing … shouts? Were they from the ghosts in her head? No, yes, perhaps …

Her kaleidoscope mind was fast-forwarding the video in her head; she was back in her parents' house; no, back in the woods collecting kindling; no, seeing her brother's foetus roasting, and the memories made her heart even deadlier.

She gazed at Zerac beside her and saw a blackened scorch mark on his silk shirt … a burn. Was it her charred parents, or a baby; was it the flames curling around her wallpaper …?

Zerac's cigar had burnt his shirt and she suddenly swooped on the burning cigar like a bird seeing a tasty worm. She picked it up as it smouldered, glaring at its bright tip. Then, giggling half-hysterically, she bent down over Zerac, who was only half conscious and weak and made no protest as she rifled through the pocket of his trousers. She took out the hip flask of whisky and his heavy, gold, engraved lighter. It made her smirk to think that this expensive lighter was going to help her end Zerac's days. Next, sitting on the floor of the basket, she tore a strip from Zerac's shirt, dipped the material into the whisky and then held the lighter's flame to the wet material until flames entwined along its length.

Kneeling, she leaned over the nearly unconscious Zerac. His features were unrecognisable. Blood was already congealing around his empty eye socket, and layers of cuts and peeling skin like ribbons blended around his one ferret eye and across his cheek. Alicia poked her long manicured finger into his eye, and when he let out a howling screech she dropped the burning material into his mouth. She held his jaw shut and flames seemed to flare from his nostrils like a dragon as he tried weakly to snatch at her blood-soaked hands, but the pain made him slip into unconsciousness.

Alicia calmly poured the remains of the whisky over Zerac and this time lit his shirt. He went up like Guy Fawkes on Bonfire Night, the heat searing her body and singeing her hair, making her move sharply backwards. As Alicia straightened up away from the heat … she heard those voices again. This time booming loudly and distinctly, 'Get out. Jump! Out!' And suddenly she was back in the real world where the flames danced their dance, turning Zerac's shirt and then his chest to creeping black flesh. The fire was crawling towards her and up the basket sides. She shielded her face against the heat with her hands and flung one of her legs over the only side of the basket that was not in flames.

The bottom of the basket flapped and broke away and she dropped like a startled china doll into the ice-cold sea, followed by Zerac glowing like a distress flare. Then the balloon exploded, showering the sea with debris as she came to the surface gasping for air

Chapter 24

Alicia lay between the white cotton sheets in the equally white hospital room. She had been told that they had a special burns unit where her friend had been taken. Her face was as pale as the sheets and she had large black rings around her blue eyes. There were cuts and bruises on her face, arms and hands.

Daniel had come and gone, staying briefly to make sure she was alright; he had had to get back to the children but he had promised to come and pick her up when she was discharged. She had smiled at him as she drifted in and out of sleep. The coastguards had rescued her within ten minutes of her entering the water after a call from a passenger on one of the other balloons, and just before she passed out she heard them say that Zerac was still alive but in a critical condition.

Now fully awake, Alicia estimated that it was the middle of the night, and she was anxious about what Zerac might say about what had happened. She couldn't believe he was still alive. She slid quietly out of bed, her hospital nightgown flapping around her ankles as she tiptoed, bare-footed, from the room. The nurse tending to her injuries had said that Zerac was in the special burns unit downstairs on the second floor.

Alicia crept quickly into the burns unit behind someone else and scanned the four beds for Zerac. Wrinkling her nose, she realised that none were him; then she noticed some single rooms on the left of the corridor. She found one with his name on the board outside, which was just as well as she would never have recognised him. He was dressed from head to toe in bandages like an Egyptian mummy, with wires and tubes attached to machines next to his bed.

Entering the room silently, she padded to the side of the bed and stared down at him. He was unconscious and even his face was bandaged, his single closed eye the only thing visible. Alicia poked his side but he did not even grunt. Hesitating, she was wondering whether she should finish him off somehow or just hope he would die, when a doctor came quietly up behind her, startling her.

'You, I take it, are the kind young lady that tried to rescue Mr Zerac, so I'm told. What an awful accident.'

Alicia jumped again at the sound of his voice and nearly choked at what the young doctor said. *Rescued him!* She nodded, her speech stolen by surprise.

'I am Doctor Patel, and I'm very sorry but your friend is in a critical condition.'

Alicia swallowed hard and managed to utter, 'Do you think he will live?'

Doctor Patel took her hand, his dark eyes swirled with sympathy. 'I don't think so. Were you close?'

Alicia shook her head, turning her face swiftly from the doctor towards the stiff mummy, pretending sympathy and hoping Doctor Patel did not see the relief on her face. 'Has he spoken or anything?'

'No, he has not recovered consciousness, and his mouth and face are badly burnt too. We have sent for his son. He should arrive early in the morning.' He checked his watch. 'Well, about five; a couple of hours' time.'

'Oh.'

'Now, young lady, back to bed with you. Shock can do funny things to our bodies and you need to rest until you are told otherwise.'

'Do you think I could come again tomorrow to see him?'

'Yes, I will arrange it for you, if he lasts the night. Now ...'

Outside Zerac's room Doctor Patel called a nurse and she insisted Alicia sit in a wheelchair with a blanket around her and scolded her for her lack of attire on such a cold night. Taking Alicia back to her room, she chatted away merrily. 'You are a brave young lady trying to save Mr Zerac; those balloons are dangerous. You are very lucky you did not burn as well.'

'Yes; it was his cigar that started it.'

'A cigar!' The nurse clicked her tongue and Alicia looked up at her. Did she believe her, and would the police?

'Horrible smelly things. Was Mr Zerac a close friend?'

'No; I only met him yesterday. My fiancé was poorly otherwise he would have been with us too. It was supposed to be a fun thing.'

'You are not to think about it. Here we are. I'll get Nurse Hills to give you a sedative so you can sleep.'

'Er, I prefer not.'

'Nonsense; here's Nurse Hills.'

It was the following afternoon when Alicia was taken down to see Zerac again. His son, Kamon, had come from Thailand, and Zerac had come round briefly, but now he was unconscious again and deteriorating fast. Alicia's stomach started frothing at this news. Had Zerac managed to make his son aware that she had tried to kill him?

As she was pushed towards Zerac's room she suddenly went clammy and thought she might vomit. Zerac could still destroy her life. Then the door opened and she was looking at the back of the head of Zerac's son, and she gasped for breath when he turned. He had the same eyes as his father, dark and ferret-like – well, like his father's one eye – and Alicia disliked him immediately.

Kamon Zerac smiled and stood up as Alicia was wheeled towards him. She tried to return the smile but did not succeed. Instead tears blossomed in her eyes and to her amazement she started sobbing. It was not out of sympathy for Kamon but out of exhaustion from fear, but to him and the nursing staff she seemed overwhelmed with sorrow.

'We will leave you two together,' one of the nurses said, giving her a box of tissues, and they left.

Kamon, looking deeply upset at Alicia's distress, slipped his arm around her shoulders. Alicia had a hard job not to throw it off. Inhaling slowly several times, she got herself under control. 'I hear he is no better,' she sniffed.

Kamon sank back down into the chair beside his father's bed and shook his head. 'I have you to thank for him being alive at all, I understand.' His English was perfect, just like the cream silk suit he wore and his brown calf-leather shoes. 'Are you up to telling me what happened?'

Alicia nodded. *Well, here goes with the lies.* Would she be believed?

'We had only been in the balloon for about ten minutes. Your father brought a bottle of champagne and asked me to undo it while he got the glasses.' Alicia stopped and gazed at Kamon. Did he already know the truth and was he testing her? No; his face seemed to be expressing honest interest. 'It was my fault ... The champagne went everywhere and your father slipped on it. There was broken glass everywhere and I think he banged his head and his cigar seemed to suddenly ignite and ... I'm not sure, it all happened so quickly. I tried to help him up but he was on fire so rapidly and I thought he was dead ...'Alicia ended with the one genuine truth.

'You were not to blame,' Kamon said, wearily shaking his mop of raven black hair. 'Him and champagne, he could never resist the stuff. It's sort of fitting.'

'Is it?' Alicia said, mystified.

Kamon's eyes went shiny. 'Please excuse me. I need to go and get some coffee. It was a long flight.' He bowed and left the room hurriedly. Alicia sat rigid in her wheelchair in the silence. She was trembling. She sat on her hands to try to stop them shaking.

A strangled moan came from Zerac. Alicia was at his bedside in a flash. His one eye was open, wandering about in his head like a lost star, until he saw her and then it blazed like a furnace. Alicia, glancing about her like a wild animal

Loving a war child

in danger, bent roughly close to his ear and said quietly, 'I'm not sure if you can hear but I was the one who assassinated your two sons, your parents, your sister and most of your relatives after you murdered my family when I found out what your "business" was. And if I find out your Thai son Kamon, whom I have just met, is in the same sick trade, I give you this promise – that I intend to exterminate him and all of your Thai family, and any others that are involved too.'

Zerac went stiff, his eye bright like an overflowing volcano, and Alicia saw his bandaged hand clench; he had heard her! 'I'll see you in hell,' she added, and he gazed into her eyes and saw the flames of hell dancing. She watched his life flow away like a river.

For a moment Alicia sat statue-still, trying to breathe. This man had been responsible for his own death. He had changed her forever. She had thought his death would make her feel refreshed, but she felt a weariness creep over her, dragging upon her heart like a leaden weight. Then she became aware of her position and ran to the door shouting for help.

Of course, they were too late to even try and resuscitate him, but it was agreed not to try. Alicia told them that his eye had fluttered open and he had tried to grip her hand, maybe thanking her; then his eye rolled and she ran for help. Lies were coming so easily to her; they spilled out of her mouth without her even thinking about it. Yes, that man had changed her for all eternity.

Chapter 25

Alicia's lies continued until she practically believed them herself. When she was interviewed by the police she told the same tale and claimed she didn't know what had happened because it was so quick. For some unknown reason she could not stop crying when questioned; she also sobbed at night and when anyone spoke to her. The doctors thought that was quite natural after the shock of the accident, and after five days they decided that, as her injuries were minor, she would recover better at home with her family.

Alicia eventually realised that she was grieving for her dead family now that her hatred for Zerac had gone. Daniel phoned to say that he was coming to pick her up and take her home. But his tone on the phone was cold and he was making an obvious effort to be polite. This added to Alicia's misery. She considered Daniel to be her roots, her future and her reason to live. Were they slowly evaporating?

Kamon came to visit her every day, which she at first found shattering, pretending to like him, then irritating. He excused his visits by saying that he was sorting out his father's paperwork so that he could take his remains back to Thailand after the autopsy. Alicia had at first been anxious about what they might find at the autopsy, but when the day came she felt too tired to care. The day after the autopsy, the police came to question her again.

'Now that it has been a few days, we wondered if you could maybe clear up a few puzzling questions,' said Detective Inspector Collins with a smile. 'Firstly, there was glass found in the back of Mr Zerac's head.'

'I think he fell on the bottle of champagne when we both slipped after I dropped it. I remember seeing it broken on the floor of the basket.'

'And the inside of his mouth was all burnt.'

Alicia shook her head and tears started trickling down her face. She was going to jail for murder!

'His shirt seemed to catch fire and I tried to put it out; that's how my fingers got scorched. I had nothing to cover him with to smother the flames. They shot up his body ... up his face ... I remember seeing flames come out of his nose like a dragon.' And Alicia gave a real shudder as she recalled the sight.

'Mmm. Champagne does not usually burn as fiercely as that.'

'I think it was the whisky. He had a hip flask and was drinking from that too. He offered it to me but I don't like whisky. That's when he said it was a good job he had brought the bottle of champagne and asked me to open it while he got the glasses.'

'Is that when his eye got removed from its socket?' the detective suddenly threw in. 'Did the cork hit his eye although he had glass in his face?'

'No. I'm sure the cork flew up in the air with the champagne. When we slipped there seemed to be broken glass and flames everywhere. I thought his eye was burnt, not gone.'

'When did you think that?'

'When I saw him in hospital. I'm sure his face was all burnt. I saw it burn.' Alicia sat rigid. She was too tired for all this. Should she just confess?

Instantly it was over. 'Well, OK. We are satisfied it was an accident, so you can go home, but you must return in three weeks for the inquest.' Inspector Collins got up from beside Alicia's bed and patted her hand, his eyes soft with concern for her.

As Daniel drove along the grassy lanes in silence, Alicia leant her head back against the headrest and sighed. Tears hung in the corners of her eyes like pearl drops; the beating of her heart was like a drum and her mind like a black maelstrom.

At last Daniel burst out, 'Tell me what happened, and I want the truth. I know you killed him. That is why you drugged me.'

'I think we had better stop, then.'

Daniel swung the car over to the side and parked, turning off the engine.

Neither of them spoke.

After a minute Daniel said quietly, 'You meant to kill him. You had it planned, and that is why you drugged me, so I wouldn't be there.'

'I didn't have it planned. He wanted me for his mistress, he said, and he threatened your life and the children's if I did not go home with him to Thailand. Then he said he would "save" Adanna because she was "just the right age". And you would have been dead if you had come. He was planning an "accident" for you.'

'Maybe not; perhaps I would have been the one to kill him, if he needed to be killed.'

Alicia gave a snort. 'You would have hesitated; you are wondering even now if he needed to be killed. You save lives, not end lives, and your hesitation would have meant your death.'

'Well, you didn't hesitate, did you?'

'He was going to rape me! It was self-defence.'

'What, in a balloon?' Daniel shook his head. 'I just don't know you at all, Alicia.'

'I told you that a long time back.'

Again there was silence, Daniel gazing down into his lap.

'What was I supposed to do?' Tears were sparkling in the corners of her blue eyes. 'It was you and the children or him!'

'We could have told the police.'

Again Alicia snorted. 'He is much too smart for that. No one heard his threats except me. What evidence did I have? And you would all have been dead the next day!'

'Yes, no one did hear his threats except you.' Daniel looked up, searching Alicia's face.

Alicia recoiled. 'You don't believe me.'

'Well, you wanted him dead for a long time.'

'I did, and for a split second I thought I could forget him, but he said he would have thrown you over the side if you had been with us. *And* I knew in my heart that he would never leave you and the children alone even if I went with him. He had no normal human feelings; he was a born murderer; he enjoyed killing.'

'And maybe you do too,' Daniel said, his voice cracked. All he could see of their future was disaster following her like a ghostly figure.

The held-back tears came tumbling out as she turned away, staring out at the vast fields stretching in front of her as empty as she felt.

Daniel sighed and, starting the car, drove the rest of the way home in silence. His last words kept tolling in Alicia's ears like a bell.

The children flung themselves at Alicia as she entered the house. At least they were glad to see her, she thought. They both fussed over her and they all insisted that she lay on the soft, comfy settee. Jobi raced upstairs and came down with his special Jamaican blanket that usually covered his bed. He placed it over her legs, which had Alicia in tears again because of all their kindness. Daniel just stood watching until she gazed up at him with her tear-stained face, then he muttered, 'I'll make some tea,' and stalked into the kitchen.

For the next three weeks, although Alicia and Daniel shared the same bed there was no loving between them. Mostly Daniel would excuse himself from going up to bed with Alicia, pretending he had work or wanted to watch some late sport on TV. In the beginning Alicia thought it would pass, and after a week, when she felt better and her injuries had healed, she tried running around half naked when the children were at school, like she had often done before, hoping it would entice Daniel. However, Daniel just turned away. In fact, he nearly ran away; he would call Squirt and, grabbing his coat and not inviting Alicia, take the animal for a walk....a very long walk.

The nightmares that came every night, never letting her go, were more vivid and furious than before. They made her afraid to close her eyes until she drifted between sleep and dreams, breaking out in a cold sweat. The nightmares did not produce the comforting arm or kind words or hair-stroking that Daniel used to do before.

Her tears would appear out of the blue even when she was doing something simple like cooking the dinner. On the third week she went back to work, knowing that it was over between her and Daniel. She was mentally and physically unfit, and after a couple of days she said that she was too poorly to work and made arrangements for another counsellor to take her place – not only until she felt better but permanently. As soon as the inquest was over she would go away.

Where to she didn't know, except at night while she lay hoping that Daniel would come to bed and take her in his arms, popping into her mind like a Jack-in-the-box was the thought of Kamon and the suspicion that he was in the same sadistic business as his father. If Daniel no longer loved her, she knew she would go to Thailand and stop the next generation from ruining any more lives. As Daniel's love slipped from her, her heart grew cold. Her life no longer mattered without his love.

It was partly her lack of remorse for what she had done to Zerac that was bugging Daniel. This coldness, together with the ghosts that haunted her and the fear that it might lead his family into more danger.

Chapter 26

Spain 2013

Alicia poured herself a glass of wine and sat on the terrace of her little villa, watching the Mediterranean sunset over the sea and the last golden glow of the dying day. Her eyes were tired from translating a report she had been paid to do, but she couldn't complain – she made a good living from it, along with her banking clients if she needed extra.

As she sat there, she thought about the previous evening with Leonardo. She knew she was not sexually attracted to him; she had been only larking about when he had suddenly kissed her, but his lips felt warm, and when he pulled her into his embrace for a moment she enjoyed the smell of masculine scent. Then it had made the pang, the longing for Daniel even worse and she had pulled away and laughed it all off, blaming it on the full moon.

Leonardo had been her friend and neighbour ever since she had come to Spain, but the combination of heartache and Daniel's rejection had knocked all the sex drive out of her. Luckily, Leonardo was more than slightly smashed, and he had just shrugged, then staggered into a chair, where he stayed on the veranda until morning, snoring and grunting. It was not the sort of thing she wished her wonderful seven-year-old son to see, and early the next morning she swiftly dispatched him to his own house next door.

Taking a sip of her drink, she sighed and, not for the first time, thought she should write to Daniel and tell him about his son. He had a right to know. However, she had tried to tell him – well, show him his son – that awful weekend when Brennan was only six months old and she had taken him back to England. She had hoped that Daniel would take her back because of their son and she would get the chance to show him how she had changed. What a laugh that turned out to be. There he was getting married!

Only a year had passed and there was Daniel gazing down lovingly at what turned out to be Shani. She had lived, not died, and there she was with Daniel, radiant. Even today Alicia felt the pain of that look, the look that Daniel used to give her. She saw it nowadays as karma for all that she had done in Thailand before she discovered she was pregnant, and some days the shadows would lift and she could actually laugh about the futile thing she had done.

With age comes wisdom, so they say, and in the years since Brennan had been born Alicia saw how pointless her Thailand killings had been. She had murdered Kamon and his associates with a large bomb, but for everyone she 'disposed' of she realised that there were many more cold-hearted, sick people across the world, all after money and power, taking advantage of vulnerable women and children. And there always would be. Now all she wanted was this peaceful existence with Brennan. Suddenly her eyes were covered by tiny hands and she smiled inwardly.

'Now, who can this be? Father Christmas?'

'Oh Mum, Christmas is half a year away!'

'Christmas is every time I look at you.'

Brennan rolled his eyes. 'Have you finished your translating? Can I have a snack before I go to bed?'

'Nearly, I'll finish it when you are in bed. And you can have a snack only if you have a healthy one like an apple or a banana, and if you are quick; it's getting late.'

'It's only eight and it's Saturday tomorrow. I'll have a banana,' and Brennan raced into the kitchen and came out peeling the fruit. 'That film I just watched was ever so funny. No wonder you liked it and have seen it lots of times.'

'You have piano lessons tomorrow at eleven, don't forget.'

'Why don't you just teach me? I like it when we play together.'

'I had lessons when I was your age even though my father was wonderful on the piano. It gives you a different perspective on music, having different people teaching you.'

Brennan grunted. 'Well, Old Misery certainly gives you that; he probably wrote the death marches. If I have him teaching me much longer, Mum, I swear he will put me off playing.'

'Oh, OK,' Alicia laughed. 'You have made your point; you are on two waiting lists; I will chase them up. Now bed.'

This was Alicia's favourite time of day, lying with her son cuddled up close beside her and reading to him before she tucked him up and kissed him goodnight.

Much later that night, after Alicia had dragged off her clothes and crawled into bed, she felt unusually exhausted. She knew it was the need inside her for Daniel, even after all these years, the only thing that marred her happiness. She grabbed her pillow from behind her head and, like many nights before, held it against her chest. Closing her eyes, she imagined that it was Daniel in her arms. This kept the night terrors away until she eventually fell asleep.

The following day, Alicia was cooking a fried egg in the kitchen after dropping Brennan off at his piano lesson and giving her agency the translated report. By this time she was hungry; she had had no breakfast, her own fault; the egg sizzled happily away as the toast popped up. Flipping the egg, she had turned to reach for the toast when a young Thai man with black hair and muscular arms stood before her. Her stomach heaved.

'Who are you and what do you want?' she croaked.

'I come on the orders of Chao Pho. They are very upset with you, and so we are here to end your life and with instructions to not make it an easy death.' He smiled, showing yellow, dagger-like teeth. He would enjoy her after he had subdued her – which should be quite easy – he thought, and he flicked his eyes up and down, taking in her slim figure. This brief hesitation was his downfall.

Alicia threw the frying pan contents at him. The hot egg hit his skin in his open-necked shirt and he cried out as smoking hot fat followed. When he staggered back clutching his neck, she hit him hard in the face with the heavy, hot pan knocking him out and he slithered to the floor.

He lay crumpled on the floor at her feet. She bent and checked his pulse. Still alive. Then she realised that he had said 'we' are here, and she turned and looked out of the window. His companion was sitting in a car which was parked next to hers! Perspiration started to appear on her forehead. What was she going to do, and what about Brennan?

Alicia raced to the bedroom and packed a small bag with some clothes for herself and Brennan, then grabbed their passports. Did 'they' know about Brennan? If so, they would surely have got him first to make her suffer watching them … Was he still at his piano lesson? Hoping that he was, she stuffed all his photos, his birth certificate and anything else relating to him into her bag, then crept out of the back door, locking it behind her. She ran the length of the road knowing that there was a taxi rank just around the corner. She asked the taxi driver to take her to the rental cars in the nearby town. Then she would pick up Brennan … But where should she go to keep him safe? How could she keep him safe? Was he safe? He had to be. She could not think otherwise.

Chapter 27

Sussex 2013

Daniel was humming to himself in the quiet clinic office as he ruffled through his desk drawers for the old plans to extend the small dispensary. The surgery was empty and he was about to lock up and go home once he found the plans. He had bought the general practice years ago and now that he and Shani were working together again – their twin girls were five and at school – he was hoping to add a larger dispensary.

Pulling out papers, he looked up and there was Alicia standing before him in the half-light of the evening sun. For a moment he thought she wasn't real, a mirage, as he often 'saw' her. She had left him with a sad letter of explanation eight years ago. And he still felt angry about that.

'Hallo,' she said softly, and stepped into the golden evening sunlight, looking like an angel. She looked no older than when he had last seen her. Her hair was dark and thick and her long eyelashes fanned those deep lake-blue eyes. Her full lips gave way to her familiar smile and Daniel felt the old customary urge in his loins.

'What— what are you doing here?' he asked, his voice cracked with emotion.

'I've come to ask you a favour.'

Abruptly, realising she was real, Daniel rushed across the room and engulfed her in his arms. She buried her face in his warm, broad chest and breathed in the wonderful scent of him. Their eyes glistened with unshed tears. She flinched when he tightened his grip on her slim body.

Daniel pulled away and gazed down at her. 'You have hurt yourself. Here, let me see,' and he dragged her into the old leather chair that they had found together in a local junk shop soon after they met. They had fallen in love with it as sweetly as they had fallen in love with each other.

'Still got the chair, then,' Alicia said as she took off her coat, revealing a burn around her elbow and half way down her lower arm.

'Oh, Alicia. I need to clean and dress this and give you some antibiotics. You are going to have a nasty scar; it's quite deep. How did this happen?'

'In a train accident last night in France.'

'Well, couldn't you have got it treated in a hospital there?'

'Not really. I am registered dead as from last night. It is a long story but I need …'

'I've got time to listen,' Daniel said, and his lips tightened as he started collecting things to treat her wound.

Sighing, Alicia started to recall her story while Daniel cleaned and dressed her arm.

'When I left here I didn't care what happened to me.'

'So you went after Zerac's son.'

Alicia's big eyes popped. 'How … how did you know?'

'Just a guess. I knew you could not leave it all alone.'

'I would have if you had not stopped loving me.'

'I never stopped loving you, Alicia. I just needed some time. I was shocked as well, and eaten up with fear. Fear that you might bring more death and violence into my life and Adanna's and Jobi's lives, which might even result in their deaths. Then you were so moody – always crying. I didn't know how to handle it all, especially the fear. I should have talked to you, I know, and I regret it to this very day. Then you were gone and I was too angry to go after you.'

'Oh, so it is all my fault then that you could no longer even look at me!'

'It's true I couldn't look at you, because all I saw when I did was Zerac charred in that hospital bed. I just needed time. Let's not argue. Things have changed for me, unlike you by the look of things,' Daniel said, incensed.

'I know. Shani did not die and you and she are married with two girls. Poppy and Daisy.'

Daniel arched an eyebrow in surprise. The see-saw of emotions was already back! But how he had missed her.

'Yes. Shani was shot in the back and crawled into one of the many tents that were flattened and abandoned. They were dotted all along the beach, so the rebels never looked into it. The tent belonged to a family that had worked in the mines and had smuggled out diamonds; they knew Shani because she had treated their son. They came back to the tent when things cooled down and found Shani and got her well. They took her with them to the Guinean border a few weeks later and she was registered there under their family name, which is why the refugee camp, the Red Cross and all the others could not locate her. After ten months she found out that her sons were both in Manchester, so the family gave her a small diamond so that she could come to England.'

'The project I got in touch with!'

'Yes, I found Jobi's uncles. Shani was with them and had nearly finished studying to be a qualified nurse. She tried to find me when she came to England, obviously without success; having a common name didn't help.'

'Then you got married, she looked very beautiful, you looked as handsome as ever and now you are living happily ever after.'

'Don't,' Daniel said, stroking her long, midnight-black hair. 'I was so cross with you, leaving like you did. When Shani arrived I thought, oh well. She is easy to love. How did you know …?'

Alicia threw back her thick mane and laughed. 'I came to the wedding; well actually I came back to show you something special. You only had eyes for Shani that day, so I left. I went to Adanna's graduation too. However, you would not have recognised me there as I dressed as a man so that you would not spot me.'

'A man!'

'Look, I must tell you why I have come. You will be receiving a phone call soon.'

'Yes.'

'You should sit down.'

Suddenly Daniel felt trembly. Now what? His life with Shani had been so ... tranquil. Although he often compared it with when he lived with Alicia; more often than he should. He missed the intimate rapport the two of them had had. Shani had such different views from him; her African background, he guessed.

'We have a son. He was the special something I came to show you on your wedding day.'

'What?'

'And that is why I'm here. He is in a French hospital and he has no one, as I am supposedly dead. I want you to go and get him and let him live with you and love him.'

Daniel folded into the wooden desk chair, staring at Alicia, trying to comprehend what she had just told him. A son. He had another son.

'I didn't realise I was pregnant when I left you, or for several months after. I thought I had no period because I was so upset. I never felt sick or had any symptoms for four months really, when I started putting on weight. By that time I had gone and upset Thailand's Chao Pho. They are like the Mafia there and deal in the sex trade and drugs and things, and Kamon Zerac was even worse than his father, if that could be possible.'

'I expect he is dead, then.'

Alicia wriggled uncomfortably. 'Yes, and most of his business partners. Unfortunately, they were the Chao Pho.'

'And ...?'

'Then, when I discovered I was pregnant, I was so scared for my baby and could not leave Thailand quickly enough. Unfortunately the Chao Pho do not forget, and they must have found out that it was me who busted up their "business" and killed some of their people. When I left Thailand I went and lived in Spain. I never changed my name or my birthday or age or looks. I didn't think it was necessary; it never entered my head that they would come after me. I just wanted to leave all that horror behind. I will not make that mistake again.

'Our son is called Brennan after my brother. He is seven and has my blue eyes and your curly hair, but his hair is dark like mine and he is the smartest seven-year-old you have ever come across. I have put him in danger. The Chao Pho have long memories. They found me and they wanted to kill me; they won't give up until I'm dead or declared dead.

'We escaped their first try and drove down to the French border, where we caught a train into Paris. I had no idea where I was going or what I was going to do. Then destiny took a turn. Just before we entered Paris the train crashed. It was horrendous. Brennan was knocked unconscious but I got him and myself out of the burning carriage. It was then that I realised – if I was presumed dead he would no longer be at risk, and possibly me too. There were ambulances everywhere so I grabbed a white coat, put Brennan in one of the ambulances and went to the hospital, posing as an assistant doctor. I waited until he came round and I knew he was OK. Pretending that I was dead and an angel, I told him you would come for him and that he would live with you now. Then I gave him a sedative so he would sleep until you came. You will go and get him, won't you?'

'And how are you going to be dead with no body?'

Alicia grinned. 'Oh Daniel, so practical and so naive always. I've become one of the best computer hackers around. I find computer technology so interesting. I shall just go into their computer and add my details to the list of the dead. I shall definitely be registered as dead, don't worry on that score. You must never tell Brennan or anyone else that I am alive, ever. You must have my body cremated. One of the dead from the train will be in the coffin, but the night before the coffin gets sealed, I will unseal it, take the corpse, and put it back in the morgue so that the proper family will be able to give them a funeral.'

Daniel shuddered. 'And then what? How will you live? Do you need money?'

'No.' Alicia laughed. 'When I was in Spain I was a translator and it gave us a living, but I needed a house, so I hack into rich billionaires' bank accounts and take one or two hundred pounds from their account when I need it. Nobody notices such tiny amounts. I have about nine hundred "clients" and I am still building my list. There are a lot of rich people in the world … all over the world.'

Daniel's jaw dropped open.

'Here is a photo of Brennan so that you know what he looks like. You had better keep it. If I keep it, as much as I would love to …' A tear glided slowly down Alicia's cheek.

Daniel glanced at the picture. It showed a skinny young boy, looking very much like Alicia, with his mother. Both were laughing on the beach against a turquoise sea. Daniel ran his fingers over the boy's face. 'If you do this you will never see him again. How can you?'

'Because I love him, just like I love his father. That's why I left you, for you and your family first and foremost because I believed you when you said that I am a killer at heart. You were right then, and because of it I put myself and Brennan in danger.'

'No, I was wrong. If only I had understood and loved you after what happened, you would not be in this mess. It is all my fault. All I wanted for you was love and a family, and now you do not even have that. I let you down.'

Alicia bent down on her haunches and gently took Daniel's hands in hers. Glistening tears were now streaming down her face. She said, 'It is too late for what ifs. My fate was sealed the day my family were introduced to Zerac. I've also had the most wonderful seven years with Brennan. He has given me unconditional love. He is so funny. I have been tremendously happy.'

'Aye; unconditional love. That is what I never gave you, in the end.'

'But you tried, and you did for a while until you thought your family might be in danger. You are a good man and a good father. I know how much you will love Brennan.'

Daniel bent towards Alicia and, holding her beautiful face between his two hands, he kissed her fully and deeply on those tantalising lips, their tongues dancing with the old passion. The sudden pealing of the telephone made them both jump. He released her mouth and reached dazedly across the desk as she stood up and backed away.

'Doctor Daniel Williams here. Oh yes … yes, that's right. Yes. I need to bring identification. Yes. I shall be there as soon as I can.'

When Daniel turned to look at Alicia, she had gone as quietly as she had appeared. He dropped the phone back in its cradle and raced out of the door, but there was no sign of her anywhere in the car park or on the street.

Chapter 28

Dulwich 2014

Adanna sat on her bed and hugged her knees, thoughts buzzing in her head like a bee caught in a jar. What if his parents didn't really like her? Although on the two occasions she had visited them in London they had been very polite and welcoming. After all, she told herself, they lived in an area of mixed-race people … But would they like their son marrying her? She picked up her mobile. Maybe he had texted and she had not heard it. But there was no text message.

If his parents were against them marrying, she had told him, she would not marry him, but he had just laughed that crackling laugh he had like a magnificent chiming of bells and said, 'You are marrying *me*, not my family. Anyhow, they adore you.'

'And you adore them; that's the point,' she had replied, and he had bent over and kissed her lips and she was lost before pushing him away. 'I'm serious, Zac.'

'OK. We will go and see them over the weekend, then.'

'No, you will have to go by yourself and tell them. That way they will give you the truth.'

'The truth is they will be delighted. How about your folks, then?'

Adanna snorted. 'Yeah, right. And you're not Papa's favourite person, because according to him you make me all shiny.'

Adanna fell back on her bed, smiling to herself as she recalled the memory of her papa's face when she had come back from Sierra Leone all in one piece and looking so radiant. Daniel had met her at the airport. After putting her back down on her feet he had stood back and gazed down at her. 'Oh heck, you are in love.' Just like that he had known!

Grabbing all her luggage, he said, 'Well, you can tell me all about him while we drive home.' When he found out that her new boyfriend was English and a doctor and usually worked in Britain, and, therefore, she would not be going back to live in her homeland, he was even more delighted. Adanna grinned. Papa was such a boy sometimes, just like Zac. It was that which had attracted her to Zac, the fact that he was like her papa.

She had gone to help with the Ebola outbreak after her brothers had begged her to come, and she had stayed with them and met Mosi's new wife, whom she adored because she was so much in love with Mosi. She fussed over him all the time, which he adored. Adanna would drive the short distance to the hospital in Freetown each day. At first she felt scared, the old dreams flooding back, but she had become a strong woman and did not give in to much anymore, including bad memories.

Zac, who was doing some paperwork when she first arrived at the hospital, looked up at her and stared like an idiot. He later said that he had fallen in love with her there and then. She, on the other hand, gave him a startled look and, in a crisp voice, told him her name. From then on he had pursued her, making excuses to ask for her opinion or help, but she remained aloof until one day as they were walking down a hospital corridor, they saw a boy of about ten hitting his sister, who was crouched in the corner trying to protect herself from his blows. Zac, who was tall and broad like a bear, scooped the lad up and tucked him under his arm as if he was a small bug. With a glance at Adanna he nodded towards the small sobbing girl, and marched to the end of the corridor with the boy squirming under his arm. When he set the kid down on his feet again the youngster tried to run, but Zac, more athletic than he looked, caught his arm.

'Now, listen here young man, you do *not* hit girls.' The lad hung his head. 'I know girls can be annoying sometimes. I have two sisters,' the boy looked up at Zac with curiosity now, 'but you must never hit them. Girls are the sweetest and most loving creatures on this earth if you are kind to them and …'

Adanna, her eyes wide, heard in her mind her birth father saying the same thing to her brothers. Zac continued his lecture to the boy, and Adanna fell in love at that very instant.

Now, as she lay on her bed thinking about it, she remembered Alicia, all those many years ago before she left, telling her that love hits you like a virus when you least expect it. It certainly did. A virus she never wanted to be cured of. She had gone to her homeland to help in the Ebola crisis and come home with a virus, a love virus, and her love for Zac had grown and grown, especially after she had told him her past and he had said it made no difference to how much he loved her. Adanna had wondered if she could love him properly, physically, but Zac had been confident that she would.

'It will happen,' he had told her positively, 'because it is all part of you loving me.' Her love had bloomed slowly until she wanted him passionately, and he had been wonderful, patient and gentle.

The night it happened they were kissing and caressing. His gentleness was so seductive that it dawned on Adanna that she had an ache between her thighs and a gnawing in her stomach that told her she wanted Zac, all of him. She whispered that she was ready for him. He asked if she was sure, and when she nodded, he slowly undressed her, kissing every inch of her body until she was nearly crying out with desire. Every part of Zac's lovemaking was a different experience from the sexual abuse she had endured in the past – this was a loving experience instead.

Zac, who had had many previous girlfriends to guide his lovemaking, some of them older than him, used all his expertise in the art of love that night. He hoped his skill would make lovemaking a wanted pleasure for Adanna – and it did. Ever since that night her enthusiasm for sexual delights had matched his.

Two months after she went back to England he followed her and they moved in together. Now, a year later, they were nearly engaged and Adanna was even feeling broody. This really amazed her, as before she met Zac she had filled her life with study and work – she wanted to specialise in paediatrics – with no thought of ever having children. She thought she would never have children herself, even though she dearly loved them, especially her twin sisters now Shani had come back into Daniel's life … and there was Brennan. Pure love at the thought of him flowed through her blood.

Alicia's departure had left an empty hole in Adanna's life. Alicia had been more than a substitute mother or counsellor; she had been her best friend. After the balloon accident she had had to go away, she had explained, because she had enemies who could put the family in danger. And although Adanna had not really understood, she did realise how much Alicia loved them all and what she was sacrificing because she did.

Chapter 29

Sussex – Christmas

It was a crazy Friday morning and everyone was supposed to be getting ready for school. Shani stood at the kitchen door howling with laughter because Daniel had his hands over his ears while he tried to concentrate on reading his letters and eating a piece of toast. Jobi had his music playing at full blast upstairs, Daisy was plonking maddeningly away on the piano in the next room, and Brennan and Poppy were annoying each other as usual. Poppy suddenly ran into her mother, who was gingerly placing a papier mâché reindeer's head into a paper sack. Shani and the sack spun up against the wall, swiftly followed by Brennan chasing Poppy, who dived onto her father's lap.

'Steady,' said Shani, and dropped the head quickly into the sack.

Daniel's letters flew into the air as he bumped heads with Poppy, and he looked at Shani. *Why*, he thought, *does Shani never get flustered?*

'Dad,' shouted Poppy, 'Dad,' and nearly twisted her father's head off as her two tiny hands turned his face to look at her.

'Yes, Poppy, what do you want?'

'Brennan says my show today is babyish.'

Daniel glanced at Brennan, who was grinning impishly. He looked so much like Alicia. 'He is just teasing you; take no notice. Your show is going to be wonderful, otherwise I would not be coming to watch it this afternoon, would I, sweet?'

Poppy stuck her tongue out at Brennan, now standing nearby, and he shot his hand out to try and catch her tongue in his fingers. She erupted into giggles and slipped off her father's lap, backing away from Brennan and popping her tongue in and out until Brennan laughed and called her a baby. Poppy flew at him like a demented spider, her skinny six-year-old torso rounded, her arms extended and the fingers of her hands held like claws.

Brennan, now a wiry, strong mean machine (his words if you called him skinny) of nine years, grasped Poppy's hands and irksomely dragged her across the kitchen floor singing – well, la la laaing – a waltz as he made her dance with him. This was too much for old Squirt, who had been curled up in his basket until the pair started dancing. Now he got up on his old arthritic legs and joined in, barking.

Daniel shook his head, gathered up his papers and stuffed the remains of the toast into his mouth. 'That's enough, Squirt,' he shouted over the din. Squirt took no notice, jumped up at the children, who caught his two front legs and encouraged him to dance with them. If Daniel hadn't known better he would have thought that the pair had the same mother, they were so alike in nature. Daisy was so different from Poppy – quiet, clever, graceful …

Poppy screamed abruptly as she tripped over the shoes Jobi had left lying about. She almost knocked against the cabinet and was only saved from falling (a full-time hobby of hers) by Brennan dropping Squirt's paws and clutching her tighter.

Just then Jobi staggered into the kitchen. 'Where's my shoes? Oh, there.' He shoved them onto his feet, treading the backs down until they sprung back up and he could walk properly in them. 'Bye, Dad.' He kissed Daniel's cheek. He was nearly as tall as his father. 'Bye, you two. Bye, Squirt.'

'Bye,' yelled Brennan and Poppy together, and Squirt wagged his tail and followed Jobi into the hall.

Peering down at Poppy and Brennan, Daniel wondered why they could never do anything normally or quietly, even speaking. If they weren't covered in some sort of dirt or paint or singing loudly they were arguing. When he mentioned this one day to Shani, all she did was give him a quizzical look and say, 'Well, what DNA have they in common?' suggesting – him! No way was he anything like these two little alien creatures by nature!

'That's it, I'm off. See you later at two this afternoon.'

'No, Dad,' shouted Poppy, and Daniel groaned and twisted around to look at her, nearly knocking her over again as she was just behind him.

'You have to be there *by* two.'

'Yes, right. That is what I meant. Where's your mother?'

'Here,' Shani called, holding the front door open and giving him his jacket, a small box of sandwiches and his leather bag. Then, spotting the papers in his hand, she calmly took them from him, opened the bag and slipped them in, closing the bag and kissing him at the same time.

'How do you do it? This is a madhouse except for you.'

'And you love every bit of it.' And so she did. 'Go on, Daniel. I have packed you some sandwiches as you will not have time to buy lunch. You have to be at the school at one thirty or there will be no room to park. Squirt, come in now.'

As she shut the door she chuckled to herself at what Daniel had just said to her. She was as happy as sunlight with Daniel, although living with him in England was very different from her family life in Africa. It was just like the fairy tale Daniel had promised her way back in the hospital compound before they were separated. She lived in a fairy castle with all mod cons, and Daniel was very caring. He looked after her well and made her feel safe. Even the awful flashbacks to her shooting and the overwhelming fear that had been present all the time in Africa had gone. Plus, she had two more beautiful daughters. They helped to heal the hole inside her where her dead daughter, Jobi's mother, had been.

Jobi had turned into a fine boy and she was extremely proud of him – as proud as she was of her two sons. They were safe and living a life that she could never had dreamt for them even in her wildest dreams. Her eldest was still in Manchester; he was buying his own house. A year ago he had married a fine girl and he had a high-paying job as an IT consultant. Her younger son had astounded everyone by becoming a pilot and working out of Gatwick for BA. He also lived, when he was at home, in a cottage just down the road in their village, with, from what Shani could make out, a different girl each time he came home; he was so African. She laughed inwardly as she recalled the many conversations she had had with Daniel over her son's 'promiscuous' ways, as he called them.

As she picked up the breakfast dishes and placed them in the dishwasher, she wondered if Daniel would ever 'cheat', as he had called it once. She had laughed out loud at his English morality. Although she loved England, even the cold, she found the people a little strange. They had such a lot to be grateful for, but still they moaned. She missed the happy, carefree attitude found in her homeland before the war. However, she was so grateful to Daniel that she tried hard to make his days and nights as pleasant as possible. Luckily he was very easy to please. She grinned to herself. Pushing the start button on the dishwasher, she went upstairs to make the beds and tidy herself up before going to the twins' school.

As he drank a coffee in a break from his surgery appointments, Daniel unwrapped the parcel he had ordered for Shani's Christmas present. A ruby pendant, her birth stone. Delighted with the jewellery, he placed it in the bottom drawer of his desk, and as he did so he wondered where Alicia would be at Christmas.

He felt a now-familiar hollow inside his heart every time he thought about Alicia – which he did every day. He felt sad, especially when he was happy with their son and Shani and his family. Maybe it was guilt.

Life with Shani was good except for his pining over Alicia. Shani was still magical and their love life was satisfying; she was loving and experimental. She charmed him just like she did while they were in Africa. But he had not been the same since Alicia and after she had left Brennan with him. His brooding was getting worse every day. He knew it was because he had these vivid imaginings about Alicia being unhappy or worse. He also missed the fire between them in bed and the familiarity that he had had with her until that final month.

Last night he had kissed Shani's ebony backbone, attending to each vertebra until she had goose bumps and was wriggling with sensuous shivers, making him chuckle. He gave her one more open-mouthed caress and suddenly Alicia slipped into his mind. He remembered the taste of her, a taste he savoured and had never forgotten. Luckily Shani was fed with lust by Daniel's kisses, her heart thundering and her senses reeling. She stroked his back and cradled his buttocks, making his groin tighten; she threw him a devilish grin and Alicia disappeared from his thoughts.

Daniel arrived at the school just before one thirty and just managed to get the last parking bay. He strolled into the building, taking in the sweet smell of mince pies, his favourite. They were piled on plates on a long table, mmm, two together with an empty glass that would be filled with your choice of wine all for two pounds. How civilised, thought Daniel. Just what he needed. And all the money collected would go towards the school funds. He handed over his two pounds to slim young Mrs Dwight, who taught Poppy and Daisy, and his glass was filled with red wine at his request.

'How about a raffle ticket? Only a pound for five, Doctor Williams; lovely prizes,' asked a woman in her late forties. Daniel couldn't help noticing her unusual green eyes. He nodded, putting down his plate and glass, and handed over another two pounds.

'I'll have ten, please.'

'Ah, thanks, Doctor Williams.' When he passed over the money, brushing her fingers lightly, his hand tingled.

Something about her seemed ... Daniel mused, but at the same time ... 'You are not a patient of mine, are you?'

'No, I go to Toppings surgery, down near the high street. I teach Brennan music after school and I know Shani. You and I were introduced briefly in the summer, at the fete. I was on the chocolate stand. I'm Mrs Brown.'

'Oh, yes,' said Daniel vaguely. He had met her before, and he dismissed the tingly hand incident. 'Well, thanks.' He smiled and moved towards the hall to find his reserved seat. As he entered the hall he spotted Sean Taylor, his neighbour and friend since Daniel had moved into the village fourteen years ago. Sean waved and Daniel nodded, his hands full, one with a plate and the other with his glass of wine.

Sean was a silver-haired man in his late sixties, and he always had a smile on his crinkly face. He said it was because of his wife Sally and his five children. He was the cheeriest and healthiest family man that Daniel had ever known. Now he had twelve grandchildren to add to his joy. Three went to the twins' and Brennan's school and were also in the show. Sean pointed to the seat next to him, which was empty, and beckoned Daniel over. Daniel realised that it must be his reserved seat.

Shani and Sally, who were backstage somewhere, had also been friends ever since Shani and Daniel got married. They were both on the school committee. Shani had first joined the committee for Jobi and stayed on it for the twins and Brennan. In fact, Daniel was convinced they could not do without her, just like he couldn't; she was so damned wonderful, efficient and calm. When he had first told her about Brennan she had not turned a hair – just insisted he bring him home at once. Since then she had loved him nearly as much as Daniel did. Daniel smiled to himself as he crossed the room towards Sean. Brennan was too lovable; no one could help but love him. He had such a kind nature and quick sense of humour.

'Hi.' Daniel clasped Sean's warm hand as he balanced his glass and mince pies in one hand. 'You here to see your three?' he asked as he plopped down.

'Yes, wouldn't miss it for the world,' Sean said. 'Wine's good; have you tasted it? I got it for a good price too. Should make a killing for the school fund. They are after some more techno gadgets.'

Daniel grinned as he tasted the wine. That was another thing about Sean, he could get you practically anything you wanted at half the price. Still, the wine was good, Daniel agreed.

'Got some extra if you want some for Christmas.'

'Yeah, that sounds OK. I'll ask Shani first; she may have already got ours,' and he glanced around to see if Shani was about just as Mrs Brown walked into the hall and over to the piano. Daniel found his manhood standing to attention and had to slip his plate over his lap. He gulped a large mouthful of wine. *God, why? Most curious …*

'Who is Mrs Brown?' he asked, turning to Sean, knowing that he had the low-down on everybody, and hoping his voice sounded casual.

'Oh, she is the music teacher. She helped put on this shindig with my Sally, your Shani, Jean, Tina and ...'

'Yes, but she seemed to know me as if I should know her and I couldn't remember meeting her before. I felt embarrassed.'

'Oh, she is like that; has a memory for everyone she has met. She is a lovely person. Works in this school two days and in the senior school for two days; you know, the one Jobi goes to. I hear Jobi got into the uni he wanted. He has done well. I expect you are proud.'

Yes, not even a ghost could slip past Sean.

'Rebecca Brown hails from here. She has an aunt in the old people's home in Sorthian - the one the junior choir are visiting next Tuesday to sing their carols to the old folk. Your Brennan is going. I believe she used to be a proper pianist at one time, so I heard from Sally's friend, Doreen Smith. She was – well, still is – a personal friend of Rebecca's aunt and she remembers Rebecca from when she was young.

'Rebecca got married to some lad and they had a baby, but they lost it when it was about two. It split up their marriage. Her father died soon afterwards and she went and joined her mum, who lived in France at the time. Then her mum talked her into doing concerts and they toured half the world by all accounts for about fifteen years. Her mum died in a bus crash a couple of years back somewhere abroad. They thought Rebecca had died too, but apparently she was just injured, although she had stopped doing concerts by then because she has rheumatism or arthritis, not sure which, in her hands. She reckons she can't play like she used to and she turned to teaching. Her aunt is her only living relative, and because she was brought up here she decided to return to her roots. Anything else you want to know about her?'

Daniel chuckled. 'Why, you missed something out?'

'Oh look, there is your Brennan, trying to get your attention.'

Daniel rotated, seeing the snake-like file of junior children coming into the hall to watch the concert, Brennan among them. Catching his father's eye, he beamed his sunbeam smile at him, and Daniel wanted to burst into tears because he looked so much like Alicia. What was the matter with him? But he knew the answer; he felt guilty, more and more every day, about the love and joy he had with Brennan while Alicia, wherever she was, had none. That was why he was always 'looking' for her.

The buzz of conversation around them stopped as the lights grew dim and Rebecca Brown started playing softly on the piano. During the concert Daniel could not help his eyes straying towards Rebecca. He took note of her appearance, wondering if she was Alicia; after all, he told himself, Alicia had been the only other person who could tighten his trousers whenever he looked at her, and Rebecca Brown looked to be … just not his type of woman!

He didn't really find her sexually attractive, although her eyes were disconcerting. She was around the same age as him; her dark blonde hair, which she wore in a tight bun, was more than tinged with white; she wore bright green-rimmed glasses and a prim calf-length pale green dress teamed with a dark green cardigan and a hideous rainbow necklace. He smirked to himself; she looked a bit like a Christmas tree. He could never remember Alicia wearing green, and now that he looked at Mrs Brown in profile she seemed quite different.

Oh, I'm just going crazy! Or getting crazier. A couple of months back I was convinced for a couple of hours that some young man was Alicia disguised. Anyway, this woman is older and has an aunt – Sally's friend – who knows her. Alicia has no relatives and was brought up in Devon.

The concert was funny, mostly because the children forgot their lines or what they were supposed to do. One small boy needed the toilet in the middle of his one line and told the audience so, which had them in stitches. Poppy, cast as a jester, jumped all over the stage and told jokes, and Daisy as Mary remembered all of her long script and brought a serene quality to the role. Poppy, being the star that she was, now dressed as an angel, sang 'Silent Night' all by herself, bringing the concert to an end. Daniel and the audience were in tears from its sweetness.

Suddenly Shani was beside him, laughing and handing him a tissue. 'You old softie,' she said, kissing his damp cheek, her love for him going into overdrive.

'Not so much of the old. I'm not the only one. Take a look around. Just because you have seen her singing before in rehearsals ...'

Shani nodded. 'She is good. Rebecca said that it would probably have this effect on the audience, and she reckons it will be the same when Brennan does his solo in the care home next Tuesday. They both have sweet voices, look so pure and have the confidence to go with it all. So maybe you had better not go to that.'

'Yeah, as if I'd miss it. I'm not ashamed to be seen crying. I feel very proud of Poppy and Daisy today.' And, as he made a quarter turn to see if he could see his daughters, Brennan caught hold of him.

'One good thing about a Christmas concert, we get to go home early,' he grinned.

'The concert was great,' Daniel said. 'And your sisters are extremely talented. I never realised.'

Shani smiled. 'Yes, well, that is Rebecca's influence. She finds the best in the children and then gives them the courage to go for it. She is the most incredible teacher.'

'Mmm, I like her too. She helps me a lot with my piano playing. She thinks I could be a fantastic pianist and do concerts all over the world, just like she used to, one day,' Brennan said, not wanting to be left out of the talent bit. 'And she laughs just like Mum used to.'

Daniel's insides twisted.

'Well, see you in the twins' classroom in a minute. I have to go and collect my stuff,' said Brennan, and spun off.

'And don't forget your jumper today either,' Shani called after his departing back.

Brennan flashed a grin at her and rolled his eyes. 'No, Shani, I won't.'

'Cheeky little monkey,' she said, and glanced at Daniel. 'You OK? You look a bit pale.'

'Yes. It's hot in here. Let's go and find the twins and go home. Sean just said it has started to snow.'

'Oh, that will delight the kids. They want to build an alien snowman. I'm sure there is no hurry; the twins will take forever to undress, dress and sort themselves out.'

'What's an alien snowman?' Daniel asked as they pushed themselves through the throng of waiting parents, out of the hall and along the corridor to the twins' classroom.

'I've no idea; Rebecca suggested it. Glows in the dark or something "awesome", according to Brennan.'

Daniel and Shani stepped into the girls' classroom. It was hot in there too. Daniel unzipped his jacket and Shani loosened her coat. Daisy was sitting on her desk with her back to them, winding her red school scarf around her neck. Half of her long, bouncy chocolate curls were caught up in the scarf and the other half swung free. Of Poppy there was no sign.

Shani stopped and spoke to another mum and Daniel crossed the classroom to help Daisy with her hair and scarf. *It's peculiar how the girls have such lighter hair than Brennan,* Daniel thought, *considering that Shani is so dark, with black hair. Yes, Alicia had dark hair too, and my own hair is pretty dark – well, before it had become flecked with grey.*

As he reached Daisy and started lifting her trapped hair, he saw that Poppy was sitting on the floor behind the desk having her shoes put on by Rebecca Brown. Rebecca had taken her cardigan off and there was a large silvery scar around her elbow and down her arm. Daniel felt his legs go weak. He sat down sharply on the small child's chair behind him. Just then, Brennan arrived with his shirt out and his jumper tied around his waist and dumped his school bag on Daniel's lap.

'Daddy, my hair is still caught,' Daisy exclaimed, and Poppy and Rebecca gazed up from the floor.

'Hi, Mrs Brown. This is my dad.'

'Yes, Brennan, I know.'

'Well, wasn't the concert cool?' said Poppy to Brennan, jumping up from the floor.

Things seem to happen around Daniel in a giddy haze. People moved hither and thither like insects and he, on automatic pilot, rose like a robot at Daisy's request and began to fumble with her hair and scarf.

Alicia, realising that he had recognised her, stood as motionless as a plumb line.

Chapter 30

'I have been expecting you, but I didn't know if you knew where I lived,' said Alicia as she opened her front door. Her face alight.

Daniel had looked around him, taking in the building as he stood on the doorstep. It was an old detached house with a gnarled wisteria tree climbing up the wall, an imposing wooden front door, and a drive of about hundred metres lined with trees that were heavily laden with snow. This was costly. Probably billionaire costly, he mused, and smirked. But when Alicia opened the door he felt like a lost child, not knowing if he should kiss her, this Rebecca lady, on the cheek or on the lips or what. It was so weird gazing at Alicia and seeing … Rebecca!

'Are you coming in or what?' Rebecca/Alicia looked amused as she gazed at him with those unsettling eyes.

Daniel nodded, and knocked the snow from his shoes on the step before stepping into the big, bright hall.

'I'll make us a drink of hot chocolate,' she grinned. 'You look very cold. I bet the kids love this snow.' She spoke matter-of-factly, trying to cover up how nervous she felt. She was *not* going to go away again, no matter what Daniel said. She needed to be near her son, Brennan, and watch him grow up.

'Yes, they were up first thing and nearly had me out in the garden in my pyjamas making an alien snowman. Your idea, according to Shani,' Daniel said, as if he and Alicia/Rebecca had never parted, but he looked and felt as restless as a bluebottle on a hot summer day as he shifted from one foot to the other in the kitchen. It was as big as his own ten-metre kitchen, he thought, with light pine cupboards and a heavy round table in front of a picture window that looked out over a snow-covered patio. The only thing that looked Christmassy, though, was an arrangement of fresh holly on the table. Some of the dark leaves had been sprayed gold and the red vase matched the numerous berries. Daniel felt an overwhelming sense of sadness.

'Yes, with those glow sticks the snowmen will look spooky in the dark,' Alicia said, and handed him a mug of hot chocolate piled high with cream and sprinkles. 'Here you go, just how you like it.' Daniel took it, not touching Rebecca/Alicia's hand, and followed her into the sitting room, noticing the piano in a room off to his left. He gazed around him, anywhere but at *this woman*, and tried to ignore how tight his underwear was becoming.

The sitting room was large, painted pale grey on one wall and white on two others, with a wall of full-length glass folding doors showing the ample garden. Right now it was bathed in sunlight and brilliant white snow, with a view of the grey English Channel in the background.

'You got your place near the beach, then.'

Alicia nodded, sipping her chocolate and lounging irritatingly against the door frame while Daniel looked around him. Her hair was piled high on her head in tantalising curls, tendrils hanging around her face, and she was no longer wearing the ridiculous lime green glasses.

Daniel glanced at her and immediately looked away again, turning his attention to the room.

Although the colours of the walls were cold, the room felt warm. The large inglenook fireplace had bright, burning logs in it and smelt of pine and cinnamon; amber velvet curtains hung at the windows and a thick orange Arabian carpet nearly covered the highly polished wooden floor. The white corner settee that ran the length of two walls was adorned with giant cushions in different shades of amber, orange and grey. And above one of the settees were several shelves filled with books, bookends-cum-statues and various objects. Every inch of the house that Daniel had seen reeked of a person who was not hard up.

'I like it,' he said.

'Good. Does that mean you will sit down and relax and talk to me? Or is your silence because you are so annoyed that you are trying to build up the courage to ask me to go away?' She marched to the settee and flung herself down, sinking into the spongy seat, and folded her arms and long legs one over the other. 'Well, I'm not going to.'

Daniel gulped, unable to answer, gazing at those remembered beautiful legs, clad in fine silk stockings and looking sexier by the minute. *Damn; why couldn't she have on woolly tights or, better still, trousers like everyone else at this time of year?* He pondered how near to her he should venture to sit.

'Daniel.'

Daniel glanced up at Alicia/Rebecca and moved to sit at the opposite end of the settee. Then, thinking that looked weird, undecided, he shifted a little nearer; then …

Alicia burst out laughing as she saw the bulge in his tight jeans and it dawned on her why he was silent. 'It's OK. I promise I won't bite or jump your bones.'

'I'm more worried that I might jump yours,' he said, and for the first time he gazed into her face.

'Oh well, I won't let you. And this visit is a one-off. Shani is my friend and I wouldn't want to hurt her by having an affair with her husband. We will keep our meetings to a minimum.'

'Mmm, is that so? Well, my family have other ideas.'

'You haven't told them who I am, have you?' Alicia jumped up in alarm.

'No, of course not. Sit down. They want you to come and give piano lessons,' said Daniel, sitting down at last on the soft settee and perching on the edge about a metre away from Alicia.

'Oh,' she said, and sank back into the settee. 'Who wants lessons? I don't do lessons here at home. I only have two private clients and I go to their house.'

'Yes, well, Daisy is mad about wanting to learn, and her plonk-plonking is getting on my nerves. Then, of course, Poppy cannot be left out, and Brennan said that if you are giving lessons to them, he wants extra too.' He saw a flicker of excitement flash across her eyes when he mentioned Brennan. 'What am I supposed to call you?'

'Rebecca, even if we are alone. You must start thinking of me as Rebecca Brown.'

Daniel scratched the side of his head. 'You seemed so frumpy and old yesterday. I couldn't get over it.'

'I do classic, not frumpy. I needed to change my age, and who would imagine that anyone would make herself nine years older? '

'And how did you get relatives and your aunt's friend to think you are Rebecca Brown – or are they all in it too?'

'You make me sound like some spy or something.' Alicia laughed again.

Oh how he loved that bubbly laugh, and so did Brennan.

'I decided that if I came back to watch my son grow I would have to have some roots here, as no one would suspect it was me if I became a person brought up here. First I had to find someone who had recently died and who had a common name – Brown, hard to trace – and someone who was similar to me in height and build. Rebecca was one inch shorter than me according to her passport – well, mine now. Then I wanted someone who only had a few family members around here. My "aunt" is the only person in my little "family" and she is suffering from dementia, so she does not know who I am most of the time. I pay for her care.'

'You mean those "rich clients" of yours do.'

Alicia smiled. 'Anyway, the real Rebecca did die with her mother in the bus crash. They were cremated, so there is no grave or anything, or relatives to mourn and I altered the details; you know how good I am at that. I found a photo of her, which was easy as she played many concerts, and I changed myself to look like her. I had plastic surgery in two different countries, under different names, so no trace again. I even briefly met her ex-husband. Luckily he had not seen the real Rebecca for nearly twenty years, as she lived abroad after they split up and they had no contact.

'May, my aunt's friend, had not seen the real Rebecca since she was in her twenties, just like the "school friend" here at Jobi's school that I met a few months back. She is the mum of one of my pupils and we have become good friends. Luckily she had not been a close school friend, but she recognised me as soon as she saw me!' Alicia giggled. 'Since then she has told me a lot about Rebecca's friends when she reminisces, so I am building up quite a backlog of her history. And lastly I decided to have a big, impressive house. Be big and bold and hide in plain sight.'

Daniel felt dazed again, but his heart was beating wildly with happiness at what Alicia was telling him. She was safe and so, therefore, was Brennan – and all of them, even if she was close. She was indeed another person.

Then, remembering why he was there, he asked, 'Well, will you give the kids lessons? I thought maybe early Saturday morning for the twins, then late morning or early afternoon for Brennan. You could probably stay for lunch sometimes. Shani goes shopping at eleven for two or three hours, so you would be able to get Brennan to yourself. Also, maybe you could come over for the occasional Sunday meal as you are Shani's friend.'

Alicia wriggled. How could she stand seeing Daniel so close so often? However, seeing more of Brennan was such a pull. 'It might be dangerous,' she excused herself. 'I'll have to think about it.'

'Rubbish; you have been here nearly a year and I met you in the summer. If I didn't recognise you until yesterday, and your so-called friend and ex thought you were the real Rebecca, we have nothing to be anxious about.'

'But you did recognise me. You were staring at me during the concert.'

'And came to the conclusion that it was not you. It is just my body, not my mind that seems to know. Then I saw your scar.'

A mischievous grin crept over Alicia's face. 'Oh really?' Secretly she felt thrilled that he found her presence 'difficult' like she did his. It was probably her ten-year abstinence, she told herself that had made her sexual appetite suddenly perk up and go into overdrive. She also wanted the comfort of his embrace and she wanted his smell and ... but there was Shani. 'We must be careful that nothing happens between us if I do agree to piano lessons and ... things.'

Daniel gazed into Alicia's face and his heart wobbled. 'Shani is very open-minded. She believes, truly believes, that men need other women sometimes. Her husband did; he was about to take a second wife and she says he was a good husband. A good husband to her means that she is looked after well. She thinks differently from us; it's her culture. We had a discussion about this with friends only the other evening over dinner. I can't help loving you both.'

'No, Daniel. I don't think that way. If I agree, we must only be friends. It is enough that Brennan is happy and that Shani is a good mother to him.' Her eyes blossomed with tears. Some days the thought of Shani tucking Brennan up in bed, and watching her hug him at school, was almost unbearable.

Seeing the pain in Alicia's face, Daniel leapt up, and before she knew it he was holding her gently. He pecked her, followed by kissing her hard on the lips. She tried not to respond, but she melted into his body as their tongues twirled.

'Sorry,' Daniel said, releasing her mouth. 'You see, I can't promise anything.' He held her prisoner in his arms; she felt like Alicia and waves of longing for her swept over him. Could he have both women? Could he live with his conscience if he did?

Alicia felt his hardness against her stomach. It was like old times, and the scent of him nearly had her swooning.

'How about Christmas dinner?' he asked.

Her green eyes smouldered for a second; then she looked distressed.

'Sorry,' he said again, releasing her. He was just so weak when it came to Alicia. He loved her deeply. It had been like that ever since they had met. Neither of them could help themselves. Their feelings had always been like a fire they could not extinguish, except during that dreadful month after the balloon 'accident'.

With a great effort Alicia moved away from him and said crisply, 'I am spending Christmas dinner with my aunt in the care home. Thank you.'

'But wouldn't you rather see Brennan and give him a Christmas present?'

'Yes, but I am still spending it with my aunt, and I have bought Brennan and all my class children presents. And besides, how would you explain to Shani why I was suddenly invited to dinner when you are hardly supposed to know me? I will not hurt her.' How Alicia had changed towards Shani. During all those long years in Spain she had loathed Shani for marrying Daniel. Now she saw only her kindness. She could see why Daniel loved her, how she brought peace to your soul.

'Gosh, you're stubborn. And you are right, of course. I suppose I had better go and pick Shani up now, then; she is in the supermarket.'

'Does she know you are here or did you lie?'

'No, Alicia – Rebecca, Rebecca, Rebecca! She knows I have come to see you. We were persuaded by the children this morning to ask you about the lessons and I volunteered to come and ask. The children wanted to come too and help persuade you, but Shani said no, that would not be fair on you. She thought it would be OK to enquire when she next saw you in school, but you know what children are like when they have a job waiting.'

'What is Adanna's future husband like?' Alicia asked abruptly, trying to quash the image of Brennan running around her home.

'Oh, he is lovely, and he adores Adanna. You would like him. He is a doctor. They met in Sierra Leone while they were both helping with the Ebola outbreak in a hospital in Freetown.'

'Oh, she did go back then! And how about her brothers?'

'They are both doing well. Adanna stayed with them while she was in Freetown. Mosi is a lawyer and works with the UN and is married and they are expecting their first child soon. Eban still lives with Mosi and is going to uni next term to study to become a teacher. They are all coming to England for Adanna's wedding, so you will be able to see them. I shall make sure you have an invitation and I will *not* take no for an answer.'

'Well,' Alicia drawled, 'I suppose by the time her wedding comes I will have been giving piano lessons in your home for a while, so that will be nice, and I will be able to talk to Adanna incognito. I miss her nearly as much as Brennan. She was like a daughter-cum-sister.'

'I think she has missed you too. She loves Brennan and he idolises her, as she talks a lot about you to him. He tells her about those missing years he had with you.'

A big tear rolled down Alicia's cheek. Daniel couldn't endure it and took a step towards her, reaching for her again. She turned swiftly and strode away towards the hall and the front door. He dropped his arms and wondered what would happen between them in the coming years. But somehow he knew the answer.

He felt a new tug at his heart. Guilt about Shani this time. His thoughts came and went like a firefly at dusk. He couldn't ignore Alicia, not now he knew she was here and so close … Although he really would try to keep away; goodness knows how he was going to do that! However, he reasoned, he did have a busy life, wrapped up with Shani. They worked together for four days a week. On Saturday mornings she would do the shopping and he had time to … but now Alicia would be in his house again … An image of them laughing and making lunch together came floating into his mind. He shook himself. Sunday was family day, and they would sometimes visit Adanna or she and Zac would come to them ...

He had waited, and hoped Alicia was happy, for nearly ten years; surely they could at least try to become friends? He would have to wait until she accepted him back in her life. A little longer would not be a problem.

Then he watched her hips swaying and her neat little bum in that tight pink dress and those long legs ... Oh hell, life was going to change unless he kept right away, and he doubted he could do that, even for Shani's sake ... He could walk Squirt this way along the beach and call in for half an hour. Just having her talking with him or just holding her would be enough ... wouldn't it?

He knew that seeing her again was inevitable, like fate; like the moon appearing in the sky each night. And even if Shani found out ... if they did become 'close friends', she would not see it as cheating. She thought all men strayed; she thought it was part of their nature. She had often said so. She liked Rebecca; would she approve of her being that 'close friend'? And Alicia ... her sharing him with Shani would have been inconceivable before. She would never have shared him with anyone if it was the other way around. However, she had had ten years to get used to him and Shani. Even now her morality, like his, was already slipping.

When they reached the front door they stood close to each other and Daniel said, 'Well, I'm glad you will do the lessons. I didn't want to go home and face the children with a no.' He lifted his hand and undid Alicia's hair. She let him. The colour was like soft demerara sugar, he thought, and it slid down her back. She shivered.

'How did you get your eyes to turn green?' he asked, letting the silky strands slide through his fingers. He gazed hard into those cat eyes; they shone like lamps alight with love. It made him feel warm and happy inside, and his eyes become moist. 'You know, you have made my Christmas. Finding out that you are OK and near Brennan and sort of sharing him … It has given me the best Christmas gift ever.'

'Good,' Alicia croaked. 'See you on Tuesday; wait to you hear Brennan's solo,' and she kissed his wet cheek and he brushed his lips gently against her eyelids, holding her next to his beating heart for a moment.

'Happy Christmas,' he said, his eyes shiny but swirling with love as he let her go. With a quiet smile he turned towards his car, which he had parked in the sweeping drive. His whole being felt content and whole again. She was safe and she still loved him, and he her, despite everything; despite the guilt he felt over her departure and what had followed. He would help her to get more involved with Brennan somehow. It was a good feeling; he felt refreshed. He had not had this inner peace for a very long time.

Alicia shut the door swiftly and leant against the cold wood, shaking like the first tremor of an earthquake. She had always thought that her future would consist of watching from a distance, but now she knew that it would be different. Her future was going to involve Brennan more and include Daniel's love, and – dare she think? – lovemaking, even if it was only occasionally. A love that must stay secret at all costs.

She was too ecstatic to feel guilty about the inevitable. She too had had the perfect Christmas gift – Daniel's love again. This time it would be forever, because she knew that she was not an assassin anymore. She could have killed the man in Spain but she had not.

The birth of their son had saved her.

Epilogue

Rebecca opened her front door. 'Why, Brennan!' she said, a delighted smile crossing her face. 'This is a lovely surprise. Come in.'

'I've got into the Royal Academy of Music in London.'

Rebecca beamed. 'I knew you would.'

Brennan followed Rebecca into the sitting room and, taking a deep breath, said, 'Can you give me a hug then, Mum?'

For a moment Rebecca stood motionless. Maybe she had misheard.

'I know you are my mum.'

Rebecca's eyes filled with tears. 'How long have …?' Suddenly she was swamped in Brennan's arms and they clung to each other like ivy. Her legs went limp and Brennan helped her to the settee, where she stared up at her tall son. He was as tall as Daniel and filling out; he had just turned eighteen. 'When …? How …? Your dad told you.'

'Dad knows?' Brennan exclaimed. His lips tightened and an angry frown appeared on his face. He slumped onto the settee next to Rebecca.

'Yes. He didn't tell you?'

'No.'

Rebecca gathered him into her arms, holding him close and kissing his wet face until he wiped his face on his shirt sleeve, pulling away. 'How long ...?' she asked.

'I've known since I was fourteen.'

'Fourteen! Why didn't you say before then?'

'Because I was frightened that you might go away again and I didn't want that. I knew you had enemies. Adanna told me when we first met.' Brennan laughed. 'You also make a lousy angel. I might have been only seven but I knew you weren't dead.'

'Oh,' Rebecca said, and they giggled together as she slipped her arm around his broad shoulders and held him tightly again. 'That was the worst day of my life, leaving you like that.'

Brennan clasped her hand, tears welling up in his eyes. 'You know I came and cut your summer grass since I was thirteen. Well, one day you called me in for some lemonade and you called me by my pet name, the one you used to call me in Spain. Only you and I knew that name. Then, some weeks later, we saw you on the beach sunbathing. One of Squirt's last walks. I saw the cross-shaped scar on the top of your bare leg that you got when I accidentally tripped you on that rocky beach in Spain. You had to have a couple of stitches in your leg and you said that because of the shape it was a kiss from me that you could keep forever. That's when I definitely knew.

'I nearly told you several times after that, but I was frightened that you would go. And other small things I noticed before made me think it was you – your laugh, and when you played music especially with me for fun. At first I thought it was because I liked you and just wanted you to be my mum in disguise. But then there was Squirt. He always growls when he meets new people, but he didn't when he first saw you. He threw himself at you. Jobi noticed how strange it was at the time.'

'Anyway, now you are going away and you decided to say something.' Rebecca smiled.

'Yes. I thought I could tell you now and you wouldn't flee. You could phone me or email, while I'm away. You will, won't you? And I'll be back each holiday. It won't look strange if I visit, as you have become my mentor. I would not have got into the Academy if not for your tuition.'

'Oh, Brennan.' Rebecca started sobbing as Brennan held her tightly. Eventually she said, 'I will, but you must still call me Rebecca, not Mum, just in case.'

Brennan nodded. 'Why didn't Dad tell me? Does Shani know?'

'No, only Dad. He guessed about nine years ago. We thought it would be safer not to tell anyone else.'

'Why, Mum? Why are you in hiding?'

Rebecca had been dreading this question but she had known that he would ask. Would he hate her? She could lie, but then ... She needed to be honest with him. He should know what sort of a person his mother had once been.

'I was caught up in a war. A man, who I thought was my parents' friend, killed my parents then with some of his family and his soldier comrades killed my brother, my sister-in-law and their unborn baby, so I killed them all except for this man, who I couldn't find. However, I found out his family were involved in an unholy business, so I killed them too. Then just before you were born, the man found me and I killed him. Later, I killed another of his sons and business partners when I found that they were just as evil. I shouldn't have done it and they, like me, wanted revenge. They wanted me dead. I'm sorry I murdered – I use to be a... assassin.'

Brennan was silent, taking in what his mother had said. He gazed into her eyes and saw the turmoil and the agony of being honest with him.

'If you had been a soldier, your killings during the war would not have been considered murder and later it was justice. That is how I see it, and I never want you to not be with me because of anything you did in your past.' He took hold of his mother again and they sat holding each other, looking out at the early August garden.

'Dad still loves you doesn't he?'

'Dad loves everyone.'

'The grass needs cutting.'

Rebecca chuckled. 'Yes. I shall have to find another lad to do it now that you are going away to university. Oh, I shall miss you.'

'And me you.' Brennan paused. 'I'll cut the grass later.' Another pause. 'I can also come back each summer and cut it. I have three months holiday.... One day I will give you grandchildren and you can be their godmother; you will be able to indulge them - and me in the meantime.'

Rebecca squeezed her son. 'Which first then; chocolate, lemonade, or your favourite dinner?'

'All of them. You have a lot of making up to do. Not yet though; just hold me.'

Rebecca cuddled her son tight while bursting into her bubbling laughter. Her heart overflowing with contentment.

Loving a war child